WARRIOR CREEK

Warrior Creek

L. P. Holmes

THORNDIKE
CHIVERS

This Large Print edition is published by Thorndike Press, Waterville, Maine, USA and by BBC Audiobooks Ltd, Bath, England.
Thorndike Press, a part of Gale, Cengage Learning.

The text of this Large Print edition is unabridged.
Other aspects of the book may vary from the original edition.
Set in 16 pt. Plantin.
Printed on permanent paper.

LIBRARY OF CONGRESS CATALOGING-IN-PUBLICATION DATA

Holmes, L. P. (Llewellyn Perry), 1895–
Warrior Creek / by L. P. Holmes.
p. cm. — (Thorndike Press large print Western)
ISBN-13: 978-1-4104-1866-1 (hardcover : alk. paper)
ISBN-10: 1-4104-1866-9 (hardcover : alk. paper)
1. Ranchers—Fiction. 2. Rangelands—Fiction. 3. Cattlemen—Fiction. 4. Large type books. I. Title.
PS3515.O4448W37 2009
813'.52—dc22 2009033894

BRITISH LIBRARY CATALOGUING-IN-PUBLICATION DATA AVAILABLE

Published in 2009 in the U.S. by arrangement with Golden West Literary Agency.
Published in 2010 in the U.K. by arrangement with Golden West Literary Agency.

U.K. Hardcover: 978 1 408 47714 4 (Chivers Large Print)
U.K. Softcover: 978 1 408 47715 1 (Camden Large Print)

Printed in the United States of America
1 2 3 4 5 6 7 13 12 11 10 09

Warrior Creek

1

Pushing up on one elbow, Hugh Carmack greeted this high lava rim country in the growing light of early morning. Frost crackled on the tarp cover of his blankets. Icy air, thin and biting as a keen knife edge, washed across his face and poured its wild vigor into his lungs. About the gray-ashed hub of last night's fire, three other blanketed figures lay.

Yawning away the last pale dregs of sleep, Carmack dug a crumpled rectangle of brown wheat-straw paper from the depths of a shirt pocket. This he smoothed carefully before combining it with the scanty contents of a bedraggled sack of Durham tobacco to fashion up a frugal smoke. He lit a match, let the sulphur cook off the tip of it and touched the clearing flame to his cigarette.

The drifting tang of tobacco smoke brought a stir from one of the other blanketed figures and the lift of a grizzled head.

"You," grumbled Sam Hazle, "can drag morning out of night quicker than anybody I know. And how many times have I got to tell you that a smoke before breakfast is a crime against any man's constitution?"

Even as he spoke, old Sam was out of his blankets and pulling on his boots. He donned a battered hat and shrugged into a ragged, fleece-lined coat. He gathered an arm of wood from a supply stacked against this morning's need and soon, where the fire had burned last night, a new blaze tapered up, crackling its cheer.

Carmack threw aside his own blankets, stamped into his boots. He raised his arms and stretched, a move which lifted him on his toes and arched his chest. It accented the leanness of his midriff and shaped his back and shoulders into a hard-muscled wedge. He picked up the water bucket and tramped over to the spring in the thicket of silver-barked aspens at the far edge of the clearing.

When he returned, bucket full and dripping, Neal Burke and Case Ivy were hunkered by the fire, hands spread to the flames, listening to Sam Hazle's scolding, faces inscrutable.

"Some folks can sure be full of hell and

vinegar while the sun shines. But let a half-way cold morning come along and they turn plumb puny and uesless. Ain't got gumption enough to crawl out and start a fire. Oh, hell no! Old Sam has to do that. Likely he'll have to cook breakfast, too. Else the whole camp will starve."

Neal Burke caught Carmack's eye and grinned. This was regular morning ritual, this complaint of Sam's. Yet, had any of the others beat him to starting the fire, or even suggested taking over the cooking chore, a storm of wrath would have descended about the luckless offender's ears.

Carmack took a final drag at his cigarette and tossed the butt into the fire.

"Cheer up, Sam. After this morning you'll be back home, sitting up to Benjy Todd's cooking."

Sam's head swung quickly.

"You mean we're pulling out? Some spots we ain't hit yet. Like the aspen swamp under Fire Rock Rim. Could be some of our stuff in there."

"Yes, could be. But wild as deer. Not worth the wear and tear to dig them out."

"A critter's a critter," argued Sam. "Being we're this close we ought to have a look."

"We'll ride by," Carmack conceded. "But unless something shows that's easy to get at, we're not bothering."

They had been working these high rims for the past month and a half, combing the mahogany and aspen and cherry-brush thickets for cattle wearing Hugh Carmack's Long Seven iron. They were spot branding the young stuff and making rough range count as they went along. It had been a hard, driving session through wild, rough country and both men and horses were gaunt and worn down.

Also, during the arduous six weeks, they had seen late summer merge into fall and met the first cold snap of the new season, which had set the aspens all aflame and the cherry brush glowing with a deep blush of ruddy color while softening the distant country with the powder-blue smokes of autumn.

With decision made, all were gripped with an eagerness for home. Breakfast was speedily eaten, horses brought in, packs thrown and saddles cinched into place.

An hour later they looked down at the aspen jungle which spread a great, ragged splash of rioting color under the somber face of Fire Rock Rim. Hardly had they shown themselves than a pair of red and white cattle left the far edge of the aspens and began climbing a savagely steep slide of black lava talus toward the crest of the rim.

"Like I said," Carmack pointed out. "Wild as deer. How would you go about gathering in those two, Sam?"

Old Sam merely grunted, but Neal Burke made pungent observation.

"About the only way you could would be with a rifle. Just shoot 'em and beef 'em right where they fall. Wild is right! They spotted us in a second and started moving out."

"Us — and others," murmured Case Ivy. "Mark yonder."

Case pointed down slope to their left. There a file of some half dozen ragged, deeply swarthy riders came winding past a thicket of mahogany.

"Bronco Charley and some of his Pomos," identified Sam Hazle quickly.

Carmack had his good look at the approaching group, then said: "See what brings them way up here, Sam."

The little party of Indians came on, their horses grunting with the climb. In the lead, on a gaunt bay and white pinto, rode a wrinkled ancient. His dark face was seamed, his black eyes weary with the weight of his years.

Sam Hazle moved out beside the trail and waited there. He lifted a hand, palm forward. Bronco Charley answered in kind, pulling to a halt. In a mixture of English and some guttural usages of the Pomo tongue, Sam asked a question.

Answer came slowly at first, in a monotone reflecting a resigned bitterness. Then words began to quicken and a bleak anger flashed in the old Pomo's eyes as he waved a bony, emphatic arm.

Sam Hazle asked another question and again came angered answer. Also a name which broke clearly through. Sam turned to Carmack.

"You heard? Night before last, Trace Furlong led a raid on Charley and his people. Drove them off their rancheria. In the ruckus, somebody rode down one of the Pomo old ones. Hurt him inside. He died yesterday."

"If Furlong led it, that makes it a Slash 88 raid," Case Ivy declared. "So Kirby Overton must have ordered it."

Carmack nodded tersely. "Just so. Also, likely enough, it was Furlong who rode down the old one. Favorite trick of his, riding over people. And one that could get him killed if he keeps it up. What's the rest of it, Sam?"

"Well, seems the squaws and kids are holed up in a brush camp by Midnight

Butte. They're pretty hungry, for besides other gear, they lost what food they had. This bunch is out hoping to scare up some venison. Some other bucks are over in the pot hole lavas, trying to do the same."

Again Hugh Carmack studied the Indian group. Their clothes were ragged and scanty, their horses scrawny and worn. Only Bronco Charley had a saddle, and it but a tattered ghost of what it had once been. Between the lot of them they owned a single weapon, an army musket, a battered, ancient relic that was scarred and pitted with rust, with a binding of worn rawhide to hold the stock together. In abrupt decision, Carmack stepped from his saddle.

"Maybe they'll jump a deer and maybe they won't. If they do, I'd still hate to gamble on their chances of hitting anything with that wreck of a gun. Even if they should manage a deer — or a couple of them, for that matter — they still wouldn't have much of a meat supply. What they need is beef, and a lot of it. Just now Neal said something that made sense. Case, let's see that rifle of yours!"

Case Ivy carried a Winchester slung in a boot under his stirrup leather. He slid the weapon free, nodding.

"A hungry kid is a hungry kid, regardless

of the color of his skin. Take a coarse bead at this range, Hugh."

Carmack swung the lever of the rifle, jacking a cartridge from magazine to chamber. He sat down, dug in his heels and rested his elbows on his knees. He laid the sights on the steer highest up the talus slide and touched off the shot.

Report was a thin, ripping echo across the void, and the bullet told with a solid thump. The whitefaced humped and spun around. Carmack shot again and this time the critter went down in a rolling tumble, legs flailing.

The lower of the two animals broke to the side and stopped there, trapped for a moment by uncertainty and the drag of a shifty footing. With this one a single shot was enough, dropping it in its tracks. Carmack got to his feet, returned the rifle to its owner and stepped back into his saddle.

A forward swing of his arm told the eagerly watching Pomos all they wanted to know. Grunting their satisfaction, they sent their ribby mounts scrambling hurriedly down the point and through the aspen tangle to where that good meat now lay ready for the taking. Bronco Charley paused for a few final words in which the shadow of a sonorous, near forgotten dignity sounded. After which he followed the others.

Sam Hazle watched for a moment then turned to Carmack again, speaking drily.

"Was I you, I wouldn't let this sort of thing get to be a habit. Too much of it and you could end up busted."

Carmack shrugged. "We'll charge those two critters off to winter kill. Or maybe, next time I meet up with Kirby Overton I'll suggest he pay me for them."

They reined away then, putting their horses to it briskly. For they were past the crest, and below, far beyond the up and down sweep of descending ridges, shrouded in the mists of distance and fall's smoky haze, lay the valley and home.

It surged strong and eager from beneath the black obsidian lip of a sprawling lava core. There was no gradual buildup, no junction of several lesser streams to form a main one. The moment it emerged from the mystery of its subterranean source it was complete, full statured. Regardless of season the volume of its flow never varied. It was as constant, as certain as the turning of the earth. It was crystal clear and changeless. It was Warrior Creek!

In its first sweep the stream drove west.

Then northwest and finally virtually true north, giving life to the valley it flowed through, and naming the town that clung to its west bank.

In this town of Warrior Creek the afternoon's sun slanted its last rays through the windows of Rollie Lander's barbershop. Shears and razor had been busy and now Lander whisked aside the apron and Hugh Carmack stepped from the chair and took a cursory glance at himself in the shop mirror.

He looked at a face with a solid jaw line. The nose was prominent, high bridged, the mouth long and level. The chin was square and there was the brand of an inch-long scar between the chin and the turn of the lower lip. Face, neck and throat were deeply tanned, though now, fresh slicked by soap and hot towel and the slide of the razor, check points shone coppery bronze. Freshly shorn hair was brown and crisp and slightly curly. Rock-gray eyes were well set, with a feathering of fine lines at their outer corners; lines which deepened when Carmack smiled, as now.

"You know, Rollie, it always sort of startles me to see the change a pair of shears and a razor can make in a man after he's been siwashing it in the high rims for a month or two. Good thing I had the chance to get civilized before Kelly saw me, else she might have disowned me."

"Wish she had," Rollie Lander said. "Then she could stay on with Maude Lawrence. Packy Devine and me, we're more than half way jealous of you over that kid. When she comes skipping along the street she brightens up the whole damn town. Puts a shine to the day. We're going to miss her, plenty, when you take her back to the ranch."

Carmack chuckled. "How about me? I haven't seen her for six weeks. Besides, she's my partner and I got to report the state of ranch affairs to her."

He stepped into the street and went along it, moving easily, checking the sights and sounds of town after considerable absence, knowing the ease and sense of well-being that can come to a man when freshly shaved and shorn.

It had been well past midday when Carmack and the others got down out of the high rim country and back to headquarters. There they had raided Benjy Todd's cookshack for hot water and Benjy's two battered galvanized wash tubs. Whereupon all hands had soaked and scrubbed and got into clean clothes.

Sam Hazle had decided to stay home and

rest his weary bones, but Case Ivy and Neal Burke headed for town by saddle. Carmack followed a little later in the ranch buckboard. This he had left at Packy Devine's livery and at the moment the only horses on the street, drowsing hip-shot at the rack in front of Russ Herrick's Acme Bar were the two ridden in by Case and Neal. Later, that rack would be filled to overflow, for this was Saturday night coming up, a fact Carmack had not thought of until Rollie Lander mentioned it.

During the stay in the high rim country, supplies at the ranch had run low, so now Carmack turned into Henry Lindermann's store and laid a long list on the counter. Lindermann glanced over it, lips moving as he read. He looked up.

"Either you let things get down to the bare boards, Hugh, or you're figuring on doubling your crew."

"The first, Henry," grinned Carmack. "Benjy Todd is the best ranch cook I know of, but I do believe the old terrapin would rather starve than leave his kitchen long enough to hook up a team and drive to town for a load of supplies."

"What time you want all this?" Lindermann asked. He was a spare, crisp talking, quick moving man.

"Any time after supper."

Lindermann nodded. "It'll be ready."

From the store, Carmack angled over to the Mountain House. This was a square-shouldered, two-storied, galleried building with its rear windows looking down on the willow and alder shaded waters of the creek. As Carmack reached the porch a small tornado of fluttering blue dress and streaming dark hair sped from the door and into his arms.

"Uncle Hugh! Uncle Hugh!"

He caught her up and childish arms hugged him fiercely. Childish lips pressed eager kisses on his cheek while they murmured breathless incoherencies of delight between each moist smack. Carmack swung her back and forth.

"Kelly, honey! How's my little partner?"

In the hotel doorway, Maude Lawrence appeared. She was a middle-aged widow, plain faced, gray haired, shrewd and kindly and motherly.

"I must take a closer look at the man," she remarked to the world at large. "I'd always thought him a fairly ordinary character, but perhaps there is something about him I've missed. Else why would the child worship him so?"

"Ordinary as mud, that's me," Carmack

agreed cheerfully. "But Kelly doesn't mind."

He set the child on her feet again and she clung to his hand. She was nine years old, slim as a reed, with childhood's glowing skin and childhood's limpid eyes. She was Kelly Logan, orphaned daughter of Carmack's former partner, Wilce Logan. Her mother had died when she was very young and she was only six when a bad horse came over backwards on Wilce Logan and caught him with the saddle horn before he could swing clear.

There was no hesitation on Hugh Carmack's part as to what his obligation and responsibilities were or where they lay. Kelly was his, now, to guard and care for as her own father would have done. Nor could he have known greater affection for her had she been his own daughter. On her part, with every ounce of her ardent little nature, Kelly adored this big, solid jawed man who, even in his gruffest moments was ever gentle and patient as he filled the terrifying gap her father's death had left in her child's world.

Carmack looked down and spoke admiringly.

"My, but that's a pretty dress. I never saw it before."

Under the praise, Kelly wriggled like a

caressed puppy.

"I made it," Maude Lawrence said. "She was growing right out of what she had, and she can't run around forever in a pair of bib overalls. I simply won't stand for you and Benjy Todd and the rest of your rascally crew making a complete tomboy out of her."

"Kind lady," smiled Carmack, "I wouldn't think of it. Your word is law. As the old saying goes — the goodness of your heart is only exceeded by your good looks."

"Bosh!" retorted Maude Lawrence. "I think you have it backwards. Besides, your blarney is completely wasted on a face like mine."

"I think you're beautiful," defended Kelly, with the direct simplicity of childhood.

"That's it!" endorsed Carmack enthusiastically. "Beautiful."

"Bosh!" scoffed Maude Lawrence again. "Kelly, darling, remember what you're to tell Henry Lindermann. If he doesn't get that barrel of flour over here before morning, there'll be no biscuits for breakfast."

Kelly darted away at a run. Maude Lawrence came over beside Carmack and spoke gravely.

"She can't remain a little girl forever, Hugh. One of these days she's going to be at an age when only a woman's understanding and council will do."

Carmack nodded.

"I know. But for a little time yet, Benjy and me and the other boys can enjoy her just as she is. You've had her for a long six weeks, Maude. I'm almost afraid to ask how much I owe you."

"Then let your fears guide you and don't ask, my friend." A smile tempered the reply. "Actually, it should be how much I owe you for letting me have her. She's always a great comfort to me, Hugh."

Kelly was soon back from her errand, flushed and breathless. She caught at Carmack's hand again.

"When do we go home, Uncle Hugh?"

He considered her with mock dismay.

"Well now, I'd kind of hoped you'd let me take you to supper tonight like a real grown up lady. Wouldn't you like that?"

She clapped her hands. "And afterwards, could we wait for the dance?"

"Dance?" Carmack looked at Maude Lawrence, who nodded.

"It's Saturday night, Hugh. And months since the folks in the valley have had a chance to get together. Sherry Gailliard was in a couple of weeks ago and we got to talking about it. We decided that a social evening would do everybody good. So we sent out the word."

Kelly tugged at Carmack. "Please, Uncle Hugh. Promise we'll go to the dance. Please!"

From above town the hollow beat of hoofs on bridge timbers struck up abrupt echoes. Several riders swung into the street and wheeled to a stop in front of the Acme.

"Slash Eighty-eight," identified Maude Lawrence.

"Some of them," agreed Carmack. He looked down again at the youngster clinging to his hand.

"Yonder's a man I have to see, Kelly. You stay along with Mrs. Lawrence. I'll be back in time for supper. And later, we sure will look in on that dance."

Over at the Acme the newly arrived riders dismounted and pushed into the saloon, leaving behind the weight of their careless words and gusty humor. In particular, the impact of one voice seemed to hang and linger, hard and arrogant.

"Trace Furlong," murmured Maude Lawrence. "There's a man I simply can't stand."

"No more can I," Carmack agreed crisply. "And he's the one I want to see!"

In the Acme, the Slash 88 crowd ranged along the bar, with Trace Furlong moving out by himself at the far end. As riding boss of the outfit he carried his authority with a harsh and arrogant hand. Physically he was lithe and dark, insolent and vastly sure of himself. His face was narrow, his deep set eyes cold. He viewed all women with almost open disrespect and all men with a secret contempt. And though he rode with the Slash 88 crew, he also rode apart from them, and while he drank with them, he still managed to drink apart.

It was that way now as Hugh Carmack stepped into the Acme and had his look around. At the rear of the room where the card tables stood, Case Ivy and Neal Burke were shaking dice for quarters, cigar smoke curling over their shoulders, drinks at their elbows. They were thoroughly relaxed, enjoying to the full these simple pleasures after the long denial of the past weeks.

They had paused in their game to make casual survey of the Slash 88 arrivals and now, at Carmack's entrance they marked and returned his slight, but meaningful nod. So they watched with a narrowing regard as he moved along to stop beside Trace Furlong.

The Slash 88 riding boss had downed one drink and was pouring himself another. He half turned and in his insolent way eyed

Carmack without expression. He tipped his head toward the bottle as he set it down.

"Drink?"

"Yes," Carmack said. He rang a coin on the bar.

Furlong pushed the coin back to him. "On me."

"No," said Carmack. "I'll pay for my own."

Dull color touched Furlong's narrow cheeks. He stared straight ahead into the back bar mirror.

"Sounds like you got a burr under your belt. Let's have it. What's galling you?"

Thus challenged, Carmack laid it right on the line.

"You know, all right. Whose idea was it to run Bronco Charley and his people off their rancheria? Yours or Overton's?"

A stir ran along the bar and now Case Ivy and Neal Burke forgot their dice and pushed away from the card table so that everyone in the room fell under the swing of their regard. Trace Furlong downed his second drink before answering. When he did his voice ran thin.

"Does it matter?"

"It matters!"

"Could be none of your business."

"And I can make it so." Carmack's tone

sharpened. "That raid was a damned raw affair, Furlong. Among other miseries it brought, somebody in your crowd rode down an old Pomo. He died yesterday. You got any answer to that?"

Furlong shrugged.

"One of those things. For that matter, what's one Pomo, more or less? Who gives a damn?"

"Maybe I do!"

Again Furlong showed that callous shrug.

"Don't get yourself in a lather. You want to know the why of the raid, I'll tell you. We just got tired seeing the Pomos slow-elk our cattle. We're not raising beef to free feed any gang of thieving Indians."

"You got any proof of such slow-elking?"

"Plenty of it."

"Plenty of what kind?"

"The best. Slash 88 hides drying on Pomo shanties."

Carmack scoffed with vast sarcasm.

"Come again — come again! You and Overton will have to think up something much better than that."

Furlong squared around.

"You're saying we didn't find any hides?"

"I'm saying this," Carmack asserted flatly. "If the Pomos really had been slow-elking Slash 88 beef — or any other kind — they'd never be fools enough to advertise the fact by flaunting the branded hides."

Furlong looked down the bar, singled out two riders.

"Beecham — Powers! How about it? Carmack says the Pomos didn't have any Slash 88 hides around."

"Hell they didn't!"

It was Hobey Beecham who came away from the bar and stood with feet spread, hulking shoulders rolled belligerently forward. A big man, and beefy, he had a shambling way of moving and standing. His face was loose and heavy and his eyes murky with drab shadows.

"Hell they didn't!" he repeated. "Riff Powers and me, we both saw the hides. Right, Riff?"

"Right!"

Riff Powers was lank and taut. He spoke as he looked, tight and nasal.

Trace Furlong brought his glance back to Hugh Carmack.

"Well?"

Carmack's answer was measured and deliberate.

"Either they're lying, or the hides they looked at had been planted. Which in itself is one of the oldest, slimiest tricks known to double-dealing mortals — planting false evidence in an attempt to justify a dirty deal."

Furlong's voice tightened.

"You'd name us as a flock of liars, Carmack? That's pretty strong talk."

It was Carmack's turn to shrug.

"There's an old saying. About a shoe. If it fits, wear it!"

He drained his glass, set it on the bar. He turned toward the door, then paused.

"Something else, Furlong. You can carry it to Overton should you see him before I do. Bronco Charley and his Pomo people will be coming back to their rancheria. I'll see to it that they do. And afterward they're going to be left alone. I'll see to that, too. Do I make myself clear?"

Furlong, recognizing the open danger signs, did not answer. But Hobey Beecham, still holding down the center of the floor, made as if to say something, then let it die as an unintelligible grunt as he got the full impact of Carmack's glance.

Carmack looked him up and down with thorough contempt and distaste.

"That's right, Hobey," he said, wickedly soft. "Keep your lying mouth shut and stay out of my way. For should I ever start in on you, I'll tear your damned ears off!"

Hobey tried to bristle, but the result was

hollow. He shambled to one side and Carmack walked out.

2

Evening settled in, blue with the first shades of night and crisp with the autumn-chilled breath of the high rim country. Opposite the center of town there was a shallows in the creek where the flow quickened and tumbled, and during the warm, sun-lit hours of the day the sound of it laid a drowsy murmur against the background of the town's leisurely pace. With the approach of night, however, the voice of the riffling waters seemed to sharpen and throw out a colder echo.

Hugh Carmack stood for a moment on the porch of the Mountain House, noting these subtle factors of his surroundings and relishing the flavor of them before going inside, where he had a nod and an easy, "Evening, Tip!" for partially crippled Tip Marvin, who clerked for Maude Lawrence and helped in odd chores about the place.

From his perch behind the register counter, Tip ducked a round head.

"Evening, Hugh. Your supper partner is waiting for you, restless as a cricket. She'll do you proud."

"She's growing up on us too fast, Tip," Carmack said. "Be a young lady before we know it."

He turned from the lobby into the dining room and found Kelly Logan waiting there. He was prepared to take places at the long center table, but Kelly led him to a small side one, ready for two.

"I set it myself," she explained shyly.

"Did you now!" Carmack marveled. "Nobody could have done it better."

Gravely he held her chair for her, then took an opposite one, facing the arched entrance of the room. He looked across at his companion. She sat quite prim and proper, her small shoulders very erect. But there was the germ of laughter in the clear, pure depths of her eyes and of a sudden she pressed her hand to her mouth, only partially holding back a little girl's giggle.

Carmack chuckled in reply. "Tell me, honey — what all happened while I was away?"

Between bites she told him, in a nine year old's breathless and somewhat disconnected way, skipping from one incident to another as she recalled them.

This was a relaxing moment for Carmack. It pleased him to listen, to watch the graphic play of expression on her glowing face and catch the bright reflections of her agile mind. She had a trick of plunging eagerly into some experience of the day, then going abruptly poised and still as she relived it in a moment of dreamy retrospect, her slightly upturned, freckled nose faintly wrinkled and her lips parted in a half smile.

"Didn't you get lonesome for the ranch?" Carmack asked.

"Sometimes," she admitted, sobering. "For Benjy and my chipmunks and Pepper."

Carmack eyed her fondly, amused at her quaint way of lumping Benjy Todd, the ranch cook, together with her pet chipmunks and her favorite pony, Pepper, as though all were her personal possessions.

"Pepper," he told her, "looked pretty frisky to me. So did the chipmunks. And Benjy said if you didn't come home pretty quick he was going to quit."

She shook her small head. "Benjy would never quit," she declared with entire conviction. "Because," she added, with childish naïvete, "I won't let him."

Other diners came in. Single men from about town, like Packy Devine and Henry Lindermann and Rollie Lander, who boarded regularly with Maude Lawrence. These lined up along the center table. Then, from the Lost Prairie country far south down the valley it was Jim and Mary Garland and their daughter, Beth. Old Jim's round and ruddy face shone with his usual hearty good humor and his women folks were dressed in their best in anticipation of the social evening ahead.

More valley folk began to show. Cal and Libby Vining, with their ten year old twins, little Cal and little Libby. Captain Rufus McChesney and his gracious wife, both tall, snowy haired, distinguished. Nellis Coyne and his two red-headed daughters, Jary and Helen. Stir of movement and a growing murmur of voices filled the big dining room. Maude Lawrence and two waitresses bustled back and forth from the kitchen.

Then it was Marty McGah who came sauntering in, and at sight of this lean, cheerful Irishman, Carmack straightened and his eyes crinkled. For here was a bosom friend. Marty came on and paused, looking down with mock severity.

"Why now, Mister Carmack, it's a lucky dog you are, squirin' such a lovely little lady. See to it you mind your manners, else it is the McGah himself who'll be after teachin' you some."

Saying which, Marty's pose of severity broke and he went on with a quick and warming grin.

"Kelly darlin', sure and it's a cute nose you have. And I see by the freckles on it that the little people have been kissin' you."

Almost, though not quite sure she was being teased, Kelly showed a shy smile.

"What little people, Mr. McGah? I never saw any."

"The fairies, darlin' — the fairies. And they are ever the sly ones, for they'll be after kissin' you in your sleep."

Marty brought his glance back to Carmack, sobering. "A little rough stuff the other evening, so I hear."

Carmack nodded. "Very rough."

"And what," wondered Marty, "would be the point of it?"

Carmack considered a moment.

"Hidden. I think. Though Trace Furlong claims it was to break up some slow-elking."

"The man is a liar!" declared Marty flatly.

"Yes," Carmack said, "so I told him. Certainly it wasn't over slow-elking, because there's been none. It is something that reaches deeper than that, offering Kirby Overton another chance to show his muscle. An opportunity he never overlooks."

Marty McGah sniffed. "Takes little enough muscle to pick on folks who can't very well fight back. Like Bronco Charley and his Pomos. But you hint at something else, reaching deeper. By that you'd be meaning — what?"

"This. If Overton is allowed his way there may be Slash 88 cattle feeding on rancheria grass within the week."

Marty stood musing, lips pursed, eyes narrowed. He spoke slowly.

"Now there is not much grass on that land, for the parcel of ground itself is of no great size or account. Yet, if Overton controlled it, he'd be right up against your line. Tell me, my friend, would I be imagining something?"

"No, Marty. It's where he's always wanted to be — right up against my line."

"And why?"

"Because he doesn't intend to stop there."

"I was afraid you'd be saying that." There was concern in Marty's tone. "And what will you do about it?"

"Argue." Carmack spoke the word with curt brevity. Then he went quickly on in lighter vein. "That's in the future. Tonight is for fun and frolic. I'm taking Kelly to the dance. As usual, I suppose you're hungry. Have some supper. I'll even buy it for you."

Marty shook his head, declining regretfully.

"Obliged, but I see a place yonder next to Packy Devine. And I must have a word or two with that smooth-talkin', scoundrelly son of Erin."

"Sounds bad," Carmack drawled, amused. "What's Packy done to you?"

"The scut traded me a bronc with a sweenied shoulder. For which, may the Saints torment him!"

Carmack exclaimed in huge delight. "I can hardly believe it. I never thought I'd see the day when anybody would get the best of you in a horse trade."

"No more did I," admitted Marty with a rueful grin. "I still don't know how I could have missed that bad shoulder. The devil must have put a mote in my eye." He chucked Kelly under her small chin. "You'll be the prettiest one at the dance, darlin'."

He moved on over to the center table. Kelly's worried glance followed him.

"Did Packy Devine cheat Marty, Uncle Hugh?"

Carmack chuckled. "No, honey. Just out-talked him."

There was further stir at the entrance arch of the dining room and Sherry Gailliard stood there. With her was Kirby Overton. At sight of these two the lingering amusement drained out of Carmack and his expression became locked and impassive.

Sherry was her usual handsome self, a

fairly tall girl, striking in a dress of shimmering blue. Her hair shone softly in the lamp light. Her features were spirited, her cheeks warmly tanned. Her glance was lively with pride and vitality as it swept over the room, moving swiftly until it met Carmack's. There it paused, and for a brief moment this glowing girl was completely still. Then Kirby Overton made some remark and she turned to him, answering him with a quick, bright laugh.

They came down the room, Sherry calling greetings to friends along the way. As they approached, Carmack got to his feet and spoke quietly.

"Evening, Sherry."

Hesitation seemed to touch her, but as she faced him there was a challenging defiance in the tilt of her head. Her answer was faintly cool.

"Hello, Hugh."

Past Sherry's shoulder, Kirby Overton measured Carmack with a poorly veiled hostility. He was a handsome, ruddy cheeked man with very light blue eyes. In a land where men seldom went in for any particular formality of dress, he was rather carefully groomed in a loose cut dark suit, a white silk shirt and a string tie. His boots were of the softest black calfskin and on his left hand he wore a heavy gold signet ring.

Of the two men, Carmack was the taller, the leaner, while Overton was heavier and carried a well fed look about him. His greeting was forced, mechanical.

"How are things, Carmack?"

"Good enough with me," Carmack told him, equally curt. "Not so, however, with some people I know. Bronco Charley and his Pomos, I mean. I'll be seeing you later over that affair."

"Any time," shrugged Overton indifferently. "Any time."

He took Sherry Gailliard by the elbow, would have urged her on, but she paused to look down at Kelly Logan.

"And how are you, Kelly?"

"Just fine, thank you," answered Kelly primly.

"Would you like to come and visit with me some time?"

Kelly hesitated until she caught Carmack's permissive nod, then answered with direct honesty.

"If you want me to."

"Oh, I do — very much. That's a promise, then?"

Kelly bobbed her small head.

Again Overton nudged Sherry's elbow and they moved along. Carmack resumed his chair. From time to time, while they finished their supper, Kelly studied him with childish gravity. Presently she spoke her thoughts.

"Uncle Hugh, why aren't you and Sherry good friends like you used to be?"

The question caught Carmack off guard and for a moment he did not answer. Then his face softened into smiling once more.

"Good friends? Why we are good friends. I just gave you permission to go visit with her, didn't I?"

"Yes," Kelly admitted, quaintly sober. "But you're still not like you used to be."

Now it was ten year old Libby Vining who, done with her supper and eager for companionship near her own age, came sidling up beside Kelly. Carmack welcomed her with relief, for Kelly's probing questions were hitting deep. First shy greeting taken care of, the two little girls were soon engrossed in each other and went scurrying away to the hotel parlor, intent on starting some kind of childhood game.

Carmack lingered over a final cup of coffee and a cigar. Others, done with their suppers, began leaving. Henry Lindermann spoke as he passed.

"Your order is ready, Hugh."

On their way out, Marty McGah and

Packy Devine stopped at Carmack's table.

"A little session of draw later on in the Acme?" suggested Marty. "Both Packy and me would enjoy seeing the color of your money."

Packy Devine, a dumpy little man with a round face and a button nose, grinned and blinked bird-bright eyes.

"At least some of it."

Carmack surveyed the pair of them with mock distrust.

"I don't think so. It would take a reckless man to sit into a poker game with such a pair of conniving, horse-trading bandits as you two, and I'm not that reckless tonight. Go rob some other poor devil."

They went away, chuckling.

Shortly after, Carmack followed, stopped in the entrance arch where he half turned, his glance seeking the room behind him. Sherry Gailliard and Kirby Overton had taken a table well down along the far wall. At the moment Sherry was intent on her food and Carmack had this brief pause in which to admire her, marveling again at the physical glow which she wore like a garment. In his eyes, all other women were drab and colorless beside her.

He turned abruptly away and went out, his mood darkening. The street was a vague, pale ribbon of dust, streaked with the thin reflections of lamp-glow thrusting from various windows. Hitch racks were well filled and the acrid, slightly sweet odor of bunched horse flesh rode the night. Pushing in from all sides was the voiceless but assertive wildness of distant butte and crest and rim, lying silvered under the chill stars.

Carmack tramped the length of the street to Packy Devine's livery corral, there getting his buckboard and driving to Lindermann's store. Here he loaded on his supplies then reined back up street to the Mountain House. He found a place at the far end of the hitch rail and tied his team there.

His cigar, smoked to a butt, had gone cold and soggy. He considered relighting it, knew distaste at the thought and tossed it into the street. He searched his pockets for another smoke, but without success, so headed over to the Acme for a fresh supply.

The place was crowded, the bar lined. Back in the card table area, Marty McGah and Packy Devine had found their poker game with Case Ivy and Neal Burke. At another table Orde Dardin and Kenny Sharpe of Gateway were dealing stud with Riff Powers and a pair of lank saddle hands from the Lost Prairie country. Standing up against the wall, Trace Furlong silently watched this game.

At the bar Jim Garland and Captain Rufus McChesney were having an after supper brandy together, and past them, Kirby Overton was treating himself to some of the same. Captain McChesney beckoned Carmack up.

"A brandy, Hugh, to settle that very excellent supper Maude Lawrence provided?"

Before Carmack could answer, a burly figure pushed away from the bar further along. It was Hobey Beecham. He wasn't drunk, but he'd taken on enough whiskey to turn him reckless and belligerent. He started toward Carmack, at the same time making remark to Kirby Overton.

"There he is, boss. He called Trace Furlong a liar, you a liar, me and Riff Powers liars. We going to stand for that?"

Kirby Overton ran his pale glance over Hugh Carmack. He shrugged.

"Use your own judgement."

"Sure!" mumbled Beecham, continuing his advance. "Sure!"

Carmack dropped a quiet warning.

"Easy does it, Beecham! Don't let a little liquor make you too proud."

Though this hulking Slash 88 rider had shown some threat and bluster earlier in the evening, he had been careful to dodge outright trouble. Therefore it seemed hardly probable he'd start anything now. Yet he did, throwing a sudden, sweeping fist, and he caught Hugh Carmack off guard. The blow landed high on the side of Carmack's face, staggering him.

Blurting an eager curse, Beecham lunged in, aiming another wide-swinging blow. This one Carmack managed to duck under. He came up inside it, got hold of Beecham and hung on whilc his hcad clcarcd. Grunting and cursing, Beecham bulled him about, trying to break free and get in another smash.

They slammed into the bar, then across to the far wall, then back against the bar again. In the quick buildup of excitement in the room there came the racket of voices, at the forefront of these the shrill Hibernian whoop of Marty McGah, followed by his emphatic order.

"Keep out of it, Furlong!"

Carmack's jarred senses began to clear. He let Beecham shove him away. But he was set and moving in as Beecham charged forward again. Lifting the punch from his very toes, he hit Hobey Beecham savagely under the heart.

Beecham stopped as though he had run

into a stone wall. His chin sagged, his mouth fell open, letting out an explosive, gusty groan. His knees wobbled and he was desperately trying to back away when Carmack lifted in another wicked one, this time to that open, sagging jaw. Hobey Beecham hit the floor in a ponderous sprawl and stayed there. His boot heels drummed and he made strange noises as he tried to get his breath.

Carmack stared down at him for a moment, then lifted a pair of hot, angry eyes and put them on Kirby Overton.

"Well? Maybe you want to take on from here?"

Overton did not answer immediately. He carefully pared the tip from a cigar and as carefully lit it. He did this without hurry, without fumbling. When he finally did meet Carmack's glance he held it steadily with no particular show of concern.

"You'll have your answer in my own good time, Carmack. Never get the idea I'm afraid of you. Beecham's judgement was poor. He had you going and didn't know how to carry through. I won't make the same mistake."

Saying which, he turned to Trace Furlong who had started to leave his place against the wall, but stopped short at Marty Mc-

Gah's blunt warning. Overton tipped his head toward Beecham.

"Straighten him out and send him home."

Then, with cigar smoke trailing across his shoulder, Kirby Overton strode out into the night.

Hardly had the door ceased winnowing behind him that it was pushed open again and Tip Marvin stuck in his bald head.

"You gents better shake a leg," he advised. "Things at the hotel are all cleared away and the music's started. Women folks are waiting for partners and Maude Lawrence says to get over there pronto or she'll never bother setting up another dance."

Captain McChesney and Jim Garland hurriedly downed their brandies and turned to leave. Captain McChesney paused long enough to drop a glance at Hobey Beecham, then lay a brief hand on Carmack's arm.

"You handled that very well, Hugh. The fellow asked for it."

At the departing heels of Captain McChesney and Jim Garland were Kenny Sharpe and the two saddle hands from Lost Prairie. These three carried strictly neutral faces as they passed Carmack, but Orde Dardin, following a few steps behind, grinned and winked.

Trace Furlong, moving to carry out Kirby

Overton's order, looked at Marty McGah sullenly.

"No objections, I hope?"

"No," Marty told him blandly. "None at all — now!"

Furlong swung around to Riff Powers, alone at the second poker table.

"Lend a hand!"

Disgruntled at the abrupt breakup of the game, Powers swept the cards into a ragged pile and got to his feet. Two other Slash 88 hands who had been at the bar with Beecham, also stepped to help.

Marty McGah, Case Ivy and Neal Burke dropped in at Carmack's side, where they could face the Slash 88 group. Though apparently an idle one, the move was highly significant, and Trace Furlong's eyes smoldered at the challenge of it.

Furlong and his men got Hobey Beecham to his feet and steered his fumbling steps into the outer night. As the door swung closed, Marty McGah's irrepressible Irish grin bloomed.

"Now there's a felly who won't breathe normal for a week. He won't chew natural before then, either. Hughie, my boy, you hit him like you meant it."

"While regretting the necessity," Carmack growled. To Russ Herrick he said, "Sorry it had to be, Russ."

The saloon owner shrugged. "What the hell! He started it." Herrick wrung a clean towel in some cold water and handed it across the bar. "He marked you a little with that first punch. This will hold down the swelling."

It was some time later before Hugh Carmack returned to the Mountain House. Along the length of the hotel porch several shadowy figures lounged, cigarette tips waning and brightening in sparks of glowing crimson. Back in the Acme, denied their poker game when Neal Burke followed the distant strains of music, Marty McGah, Case Ivy and Packy Devine had settled down to three handed, cut-throat pedro.

The dancing was going on in the hotel dining room. Here tables and chairs had been moved against the wall, leaving the wide center free. Elsewhere, in lobby and hallways, sounded the excited shouts of children and the light thump of speeding feet. Even as Carmack stepped inside it was Kelly who fled breathlessly by, dodging into the parlor and there hiding, softly laughing, behind a piece of furniture.

Carmack went on to the arched entrance of the dining room, stood watching the dancers. Cal Vining and his wife spun by, and Neal Burke with Beth Garland and Kenny Sharpe with Helen Coyne. One of the Lost Prairie riders stepped past with Helen's younger sister, Jary, holding her with such sedate and extreme care that Jary was teasing him and had him all flushed and sheepish looking. Captain McChesney was steering Mrs. Garland carefully about, while his wife smiled down at stocky old Jim Garland, whose red face shone with pleasure and sweat.

Then Sherry Gailliard went by in the arms of Kirby Overton. In contrast to the eager gaiety of her earlier mood, it seemed to Carmack that she had sobered, as though troubled over something. He was pondering this when Orde Dardin moved up beside him.

"Better get in there and rescue her, Hugh. Just because she came with him is no reason for Overton to claim every dance."

"She's old enough to know her own mind." Carmack answered, a trifle curt. "She don't have to dance with him if she doesn't want to. And there's nothing holding you back, Orde."

"Except that I'm one of the hired hands," retorted Dardin drily. "Oh sure, Sherry would dance with me out of kindness. But that ain't the point."

There was that in Orde Dardin's tone which made Carmack turn.

"What is the point?"

"Like this," Dardin said. "When I ride for an outfit, all its interests — and I mean all — are my concern. Now it happens I like Kirby Overton little, and I like even less the way he takes for granted the right to possess anything and everything that happens to strike his fancy. Right now he's doing Sherry no good at all in the eyes of other folks, close herding her the way he is."

"You told her that?"

"Hell — no! I like my job. Was I to butt into her private affairs — her being proud as she is — she'd fire me, sure. But now if you — ?"

"So that's it," drawled Carmack. "You want me to walk in where you're afraid to."

"Call it so if you want. But should you break the ice, the other boys would flock around. There was a time when you and Sherry were pretty good friends. Maybe she'll listen to you."

"She didn't last time," Carmack recalled bluntly. "She tromped all over me."

"That was then," persisted Dardin. "This is now. Women folk can change their minds, you know."

"I wonder," Carmack scoffed cynically.

The music stopped. Captain McChesney and old Jim Garland escorted their respective partners to their chairs. The younger group, the two Coyne sisters and Beth Garland and their partners, drifted into a little group further along. But across the room Sherry Gailliard and Kirby Overton stood alone, markedly so.

As the interval before the next dance ran on with no one approaching Sherry and Overton, a deepening restlessness gripped Hugh Carmack. With it came decision.

"All right," he told Orde Dardin briefly. "You win."

He went quickly and quietly over to Sherry's side, and as quietly spoke.

"The next one is mine, Sherry."

Kirby Overton's eyes went hard, his tone likewise.

"The accepted courtesy, Carmack, is I believe, to first ask permission of the lady's escort."

Carmack shrugged.

"That would imply some sort of possession on your part. Which doesn't happen to be the case."

As he spoke, the music, furnished by guitar, fiddle and a banjo, struck up. Before Overton could argue further, or Sherry object, Carmack had an arm about her, drawing her out to the floor.

3

He smiled down at her. "This is me, remember? Hugh Carmack — an old, old friend."

It seemed she clung to the shadow of some latent hostility, for while she matched his step with reluctance, she also pressed back against the circle of his arm. Abruptly that arm was steely, bringing her breathlessly tight against him as his drawl took on a clipped sternness.

"Behave yourself! Anybody would think you'd never seen me before and that my pockets were full of scorpions. You may as well make up your mind to it, my lovely one — I'm going to dance this one with you if I have to lug you around the floor under one arm. And if you don't quit treating me like I was some sort of plague, I'll muss you up, right here in front of everybody."

Her glance flayed him. "You — you wouldn't dare!"

His arm tightened still further. "No? Think not — ?"

She ducked a fragrant head against his shoulder, murmuring defeat.

"All — all right. Now, please — give me

room to breathe."

He slacked up on the pressure. Presently further muffled words came up to him.

"Just as always. A bully — a brute — !"

Carmack's smile returned.

"That's better. Now it's the Sherry Gailliard I used to know. Like old times — you rawhiding me. Wouldn't be natural, otherwise."

"Then — then why did you want to dance with me?"

"Maybe I wanted to rowel Mister Kirby a little bit."

"I might have known. Ever the trouble hunter, is that it?"

"Not necessarily. Depends on what you call trouble."

She grew silent, dancing as she walked, light, graceful, vibrant. When they circled past the entrance arch, Orde Dardin grinned his approval. Further along, Carmack looked for Kirby Overton but could not locate him, so made teasing remark.

"The gentleman friend, Mister Overton, seems to have gone off somewhere. Probably sulking."

She looked up, the lightning stirring anew.

"Keep talking like that and no matter what you threaten, I won't dance another step."

"Not even if I beat you?"

"No, not even if you beat me!"

He considered her gravely, a masked gentleness far back in his eyes.

"Some day I may even do that. Though lightly. Just to prove the kind of barbarian I am."

She twisted in his arms, sputtering with frustration.

"Oh — you — you — ! You'll just never change!"

"No," he admitted steadily, "in some ways I never will. Like the way it used to be with us is still the way it is with me — the way it will always be with me. Also, like always, I got no use for Kirby Overton, no use at all. And I don't like to see you going out with him. Which I've told you before."

"Yes," she retorted, "you told me before. And I told you it was none of your business who I went around with. It still isn't."

"Which," Carmack said wryly, "brings us right back to the sane old thistle patch, doesn't it?"

She studied him with narrowed eyes.

"There's a bruise on the side of your face. It wasn't there at supper time. You've been in a brawl?"

"Not much of a one. Your gentleman friend, Mister Overton, sicced that big animal, Hobey Beecham on me."

Sherry fairly gritted her teeth. "If you refer again to Kirby Overton as my gentleman friend, I'll — I'll — !"

"Well, isn't he? You came to the dance with him. You ride with him. From all I see and hear, you're with him more and more all the time. Others besides me are noticing it."

"Let them," she stormed. "Why can't people mind their own affairs and let me mind mine?"

"Could be because they think too much of you to see you hurt. Ever stop to figure it that way?"

Sherry almost whimpered with anger.

"Anybody would think I was doing something terrible, going to a dance with a man."

"Not just a man," Carmack corrected. "But *the* man!"

She defended hotly. "Kirby Overton has never been anything but a gentleman around me."

"With you he'd better be. But it hasn't been that way at all with others."

"You realize, of course, that you're creeping behind another man's back?"

Carmack shook his head. "Not necessarily. I've said worse to his face. And will say more."

The music stopped. Carmack held Sherry a moment longer, as if reluctant to let her out of his arms. He gave her a slight and gentle shake.

"Thanks," he murmured softly. "Now give some of the other boys a chance. They all want to dance with you."

Past that fragrant head of hers he caught Orde Dardin's glance and jerked a beckoning nod. Grinning, Orde came and took over.

Carmack turned into the lobby and on into the night beyond. At the porch edge two men stood, conversing in low tones. A half-spoken remark dwindled out, but not before Carmack caught the tone and identified the speaker. He closed in and Kirby Overton and Trace Furlong came around to face him.

"This is better than I'd hoped," observed Carmack briefly. "I've been wanting a word with you, Overton. Now both of you can hear what I got to say."

"Maybe," retorted Overton, "we're not interested."

"You'd better be!" Carmack was equally curt. "Here it is, right to the point. If Furlong has given it to you already, it can still bear repeating. The rancheria strip is strictly neutral. Stay away from it, Overton.

Bronco Charley and his people are coming back, and are going to be left alone when they do. Is that clear?"

"Oh, quite," jeered Overton. "Only it doesn't mean anything. Any time I need you to tell me what I can or can't do, I'll let you know, Carmack. The way you talk, anyone might think you owned this valley."

"Just enough of it to have considerable concern in its affairs," said Carmack steadily. "Don't try and reach too far, or you could fall flat on your face."

Kirby Overton took a deep drag on his cigar and let the smoke dribble slowly over his lips.

"Is it reaching too far when a man moves to put a stop to the slow-elking of his cattle?"

"The Pomos never slow-elked any of your cattle," Carmack told him flatly.

"Slash 88 hides were found on rancheria premises."

"That one," said Carmack, "is so old it's got moss on it. Any such hides found on the rancheria strip were planted there, with malice aforethought, as the saying goes. You know it and I know it!"

Overton's words took on a sneering edge. "You know just a hell of a lot, don't you?"

Carmack shrugged.

"I know enough not to be taken in by a flock of lies. And I know exactly how your mind runs, Overton. Even as a kid you were sly and greedy, and I can't see where the years have changed you any. I know why you ordered that raid on the Pomos — I know exactly why. So you could get right up against Long Seven ground. The slow-elking talk was just a thin excuse for you to move in and occupy. I doubt it will fool others, and certainly not me. So don't try it, Overton — don't try and occupy!"

Darkness masked the ugly fires burning in Kirby Overton's eyes. He took another deep pull at his half-smoked cigar, then threw it into the street with a hard, quick gesture.

"All right," he ground out harshly. "You've called it. So I might as well add the rest. I'm going to break you, Carmack. I'm going to run you out of this valley!"

"Fine!" applauded Carmack sarcastically. "Now we know just where we stand. And seeing as you've made yourself clear, I'll lay a few things on the line, myself. First, anything you start will shape up just as rough as you want to make it. Second, there's a big chance that you'll step into water way over your head. And here's one more little item. You owe me for a couple of beef critters."

Overton stared. "I — owe you for cattle! Since when?"

"Since this morning. I had to gun down two head of Long Seven stuff to keep Pomo kids from going hungry. I figure that by rights you should pay for that meat."

Overton exploded. "Of all the damned gall — !"

Trace Furlong stirred, his words thin and barren.

"Worse than that."

"About as I expected," Carmack said. "Well, there are ways — and ways — for me to collect. I'll decide on something. In the meantime — remember you've been told!"

The dance was still going strong when Hugh Carmack rolled his buckboard out of town. With his decision to head for home he had gone in search of Kelly Logan and found her curled up in an easy chair in the hotel parlor, thoroughly weary from play and half asleep. She had assented readily to their leaving and hurried to gather her belongings, to thank Maude Lawrence and say goodbye. Now, close wrapped in a blanket she was a small, warm bundle, snugged against him on the buckboard seat. Before they were a mile gone from town she was asleep. Carmack dropped the security of an arm about her.

The late stars were a far away glitter and the world immense and deeply black. As always during these deepening hours of the night it seemed to Carmack that a sort of primitive, voiceless current flowed close to the earth to remind a man of his insignificance and impermanence.

Lost somewhere in the vast darkness a coyote mourned, and even in the depths of slumber that far-off note of wildness appeared to touch Kelly, for she stirred slightly and crept even closer inside the protection of Carmack's arm.

It was an unconscious move that emphasized his full obligation to this youngster. Quite literally, half of everything that was Long Seven belonged to her. Any blow against him or Long Seven was a blow against her. He wondered if Kirby Overton had fully considered this fact and what it could mean in the way of opposition. If Overton had, then it meant that he was not only completely callous, but also completely sure of himself.

It was full midnight by the time Carmack's steadily jogging buckboard team slowed up beside the home corrals. A light still burned in the cookshack and the invisible scent of wood-smoke hung in the damp, chill air. Carmack urged the team on over to the cookshack door. Sam Hazle stepped out and Benjy Todd made a thin, waspy shape against the light.

"You're late," Sam grumbled. "Figured you home hours ago. That Kelly with you? She's all right, ain't she?"

"As rain. And asleep. While I get her to bed, you can unload these supplies and put up the team."

Carmack carried Kelly into the ranch-house. The movement wakened her and when he got a light going she insisted with a quaint, sleepy dignity on caring for herself, even to brushing her hair before getting into bed. There, snug in familiar surroundings, she smiled blissfully and held up her slim, child's arms. Carmack bent for a hug and a goodnight kiss, then turned down the light and went out.

He crossed again to the cookshack. Heat still held in the stove and a pot of coffee steamed gently. He poured himself a cup of this and backed up to the stove's welcome warmth. Over the rim of his cup he watched Benjy Todd stack supplies on the shelves at the far end of the room. Benjy had a point of complaint.

"Next time you're in town, you tell Henry Lindermann he owes us a ten pound sack of oatmeal. Last sack turned up weevilly. I had to throw most of it away."

"Maybe you'd had it around too long," Carmack suggested.

"Not me. Lindermann did," Benjy declared. "And we got to have oatmeal for Kelly. She ain't never going to get her growth right, less'n she has her breakfast mush regular. You can tell Lindermann that, too."

Carmack grinned faintly. "All right, Benjy — I will."

Sam Hazle came in from the corrals and helped himself to coffee.

"Something must have happened in town to keep you so late?"

Carmack nodded. "Turned out to be a Saturday night. Maude Lawrence had a dance going at the Mountain House. Kelly and me, we decided to stick around a while."

"You step on somebody's feet?" Sam asked.

Carmack looked at him, puzzled. "Come again?"

"Or maybe you ran into a door."

"Oh — that!" Carmack touched the bruise on his face. "The mark of Hobey Beecham."

"Knew it!" exclaimed Sam. "Had to be something of the sort. Well, let's have the rest of it?"

Carmack told him, making it brief.

"You stopped too soon," complained Sam. "After laying Beecham out you should have taken a swing at Overton."

"I thought of it," Carmack admitted. "Just as well I didn't. It would have spoiled the evening for some innocent folks."

Benjy Todd had been listening avidly. Excitement of any sort was a rare thing in Benjy's kitchen, so when even a hint of such came along he savored it to the fullest. Now he had his say.

"You should have walloped him good, Hugh. Yes, sir! You should have busted him! Because one of these days you'll have to. You wait and see!"

Carmack drained his cup and put it down. "You could be right, Benjy. But tonight wasn't the time or place."

"You mention the raid to him?" asked Sam.

"To him, and Trace Furlong."

"What did they have to say?"

"Admitted it. But claimed it was a move to stop the Pomos from slow-elking Slash 88 beef."

"That's hog-wash!" charged Sam. "The Pomos know better than to try anything of the sort."

"So I told Overton," Carmack said. He

paused, held by a moment of sober speculation before adding: "I argued Overton into a corner and he let his mad get the best of him. He came up with a pretty strong statement. Said he intended to break Long Seven and run me out of the valley."

"The hell he did!" exploded Sam, incredulous. "Has he gone crazy? For that could be a large order — a mighty large order!"

"Knew you should have busted him," Benjy Todd put in heatedly. "That'd showed him where the eagle builds its nest!"

"Just how does he figure to go about this little chore of breaking us and running us out?" Sam probed. "Or didn't he let on?"

"He didn't."

"Likely he was just making talk," Sam decided.

Carmack shook his head. "No, he meant it. He meant every word of it!"

Midnight Butte was a rugged cone of somber lava, lifting abruptly from the surrounding country. Thickets of mahogany brush shrouded its sprawling base and edged part way up its broken sides. Here and there through the mahoganies were clearings of sparse grass and stunted sage, dotted with junipers heavy with berries which carried a dusty, blue-gray look and spiced the morning air with an aromatic pungency. A short distance south of the butte a clump of conifers stood in a small aspen swamp, and here the smoke of campfires winnowed palely upward.

Lining on the smoke, Hugh Carmack and Sam Hazle rode in on the brush camp of the Pomos. Broad, dark faces showed and old Bronco Charley himself moved out to greet them. He lifted an arm and made guttural announcement.

Sam Hazle gave the word to Carmack.

"We're to light and eat. Me, I'm still part full of breakfast, but we better make the gesture. Be a good chance to tell him what you want. Besides, we'll be gnawing on some of our own beef."

They stepped down. Round about the several campfires, squaws hovered, and the suety fragrance of roasting beef drifted through the smoke. Here and there a few tattered blankets and other meager possessions were in evidence, but very plainly this was a hardship camp.

On all sides was the hurry and scurry of welcome, and as Carmack and Sam hunkered on their heels beside Bronco Charley, a young squaw brought each of them a section of fresh roasted beef ribs, dripping and savory.

Though a few more years would surely doom Sadie Colo to the same squat shapelessness of her Pomo sisters, at the moment she still possessed some of the grace of youth, and as she presented the portions of meat to Carmack and Sam, her black eyes were alive with a shy excitement and she was almost pretty.

A number of youngsters showed, faces shining with suet grease and full fed satisfaction, and a papoose, securely laced in its swaddling basket, swung on a nearby aspen limb. The small brown mite surveyed the world soberly out of a pair of beady, shoe-button eyes, but when Carmack grinned at it he got a wriggling, toothless one in return.

"Still feeling bad, Sam — over the two critters we beefed for these people?" Carmack murmured.

Sam made gruff retort.

"Hell, no! And I really didn't from the first, as you well know. Now what do you want me to tell old Charley here?"

"That he's to stay on at this camp until further word. And that I'll see to it he and his people get back on their rancheria before too long. Also, when they do, that they'll be left alone."

Sam Hazle explained to the old Pomo.

Bronco Charley considered it for an interval, his seamed, dark face stoic and expressionless. Abruptly his eyes flashed and he made vehement utterance, which ran into an equally vehement gesture. After which he shrugged and the fires died and he settled back in a weary crouch, further words dwindling into a fading monotone.

"I couldn't get quite all of it," Sam interpreted. "But here's the general idea. First, if he was young again and his arm strong, he'd take care of Slash 88 in his own way. But now the weight of the years rests upon him and his arm is weak. For the sake of his people he'll accept your help and do whatever you say."

"This thing could run into a little time," Carmack decided. "Better tell him to have his people put some brush wickiups together. I'll see that they get some more blankets and food."

"You're a big-hearted damn fool," murmured Sam inelegantly. "But I'd go to hell for you because of it." Whereupon he turned to Bronco Charley with the balance of Carmack's message.

The old Pomo put his full regard on Carmack. He pressed a wrinkled hand to a bony chest, then made a sweeping outward gesture, palm up.

"From his heart he declares it," Sam Hazle said. "You are his finest friend."

4

It was as part of an Oregon-bound wagon train that Jefferson Gailliard, with his wife and infant daughter, first crossed the Barrier Hills through Gateway Pass. To other members of the train the valley they emerged into was merely another of such to be crossed and left behind on their way to the fabled Oregon land. But to Jeff Gailliard, still limping from the effects of a Harper's Ferry musket slug, taken during the crimson holocaust which history was to designate as the battle of Chancellorsville, this valley in the lonely lava country was the promised land he'd come in search of. So here he had stopped his wagon and outspanned.

That had been a full quarter century before. Long since had his wife been laid to rest in this lava harshened earth, and Jeff Gailliard himself, old and crippled before his time because of hardship and his ancient wound, and made somewhat sour and withdrawn by these infirmities, now spent most of his days in a chair on the porch of his log-built ranchhouse and watched his cattle graze on some of the Warrior Creek meadows.

This was the Gateway Ranch, and when Hugh Carmack rode up to it, old Jeff was in his chair, blanket wrapped against mid-morning's lingering chill. He nodded brief greeting and made curt remark as Carmack dismounted and climbed the low steps.

"Been some time since you were around here last."

"That's right, Jeff," Carmack nodded. "It's good to see you again. How are things?"

"Kinda puny. This damn chair grabs me tighter all the time." Old Jeff grunted and sucked meagerly on a blackened pipe.

"Sherry home?" Carmack asked.

Sherry answered that question by appearing in the doorway. This girl lost nothing in slender charm in the wearing of a simple house dress and starched gingham apron, and with her hair in a single heavy braid between her shoulders. There were dabs of flour on her bared forearms and also on one cheek. She looked at Carmack with a veiled directness.

"Well — surprise! What brings you here? To apologize for last night, maybe?"

"Me — apologize? What for? Because I made you dance with me and squeezed you tight? Shucks — that was fun, and you know it." He sniffed the air. "Lordy — but do I smell good things cooking!"

"So that's it. You came around to beg something to eat?"

Grinning, Carmack shook his head. "No, I'm not grub-lining. In fact, I ate just a little while ago. Roast beef rib, served up by a pretty little Pomo squaw, Sadie Colo. But I am asking for something. Old blankets — and stuff."

"I must know more about that," decided Sherry. "You better come on in. I'm baking today and have things in the oven."

He followed her into the kitchen. He tossed his hat in a corner, hooked up a chair with a boot toe, swung it around and straddled it, resting his crossed forearms on the back of it. There were some fresh baked raisin cookies spread to cool on the kitchen table and Carmack reached out a long arm and snared one. He took a bite, rolled his eyes and made observation to the world at large.

"Why does she have to be so doggoned good-looking and such a swell cook? Why couldn't she be dowdy and homely as a mud turtle and too dumb to know a fry pan from a stew pot? Then a man could ride plumb away and forget her without breaking his heart. As it is — !" He shrugged and took another mouthful of cooky.

Sherry, busy at the stove, spoke without turning.

"Flattery is cheap and will get you nowhere, Mister Carmack. Now what is this about old blankets — and stuff?"

Carmack finished his cooky and hooked another. But as he spoke, the note of easy banter was gone.

"You heard of the raid Slash 88 pulled on the Pomos?"

"Yes, I heard. What about it?"

"Like this. Bronco Charley and his people are in a hardship camp over by Midnight Butte. They could use some more blankets. I'm out looking for possible cast-offs. You got any around?"

"Probably. You speak of eating with the Pomos. What kind of beef was it — Slash 88?"

"No," Carmack told her drily. "Long Seven."

She came around to face him, sober and intent. "Some that had been slow-elked?"

"No," Carmack said a second time. "Some that I gave them. The Pomos haven't been slow-elking anybody's cattle."

"There are people who believe otherwise."

"Claim it, not really believe it," Carmack

corrected. "You'd be meaning friend Overton, of course. But he's dead wrong and he knows it. I've said this to you before and I say it to you again — you shouldn't believe all that fellow tells you."

Sherry stiffened, her shoulders going back, her chin lifting. Her eyes flashed.

"Careful! Else we'll be quarreling again."

Carmack dropped his chin on his folded arms, peering at her intently.

"So help me," he murmured, "I can't figure it. You, Sherry Gailliard, have never been anybody's fool. You're smart as they come. In all things, it seems, except where Kirby Overton is concerned. Oh, sure — we've quarreled over that fellow before and probably will again. Just the same, there's one thing you can depend on with your life — I'd never try to mislead you in anything. I think too much of you. So, no matter what the penalty, I'll just have to keep on warning you against Overton. And when he says the Pomos have been slow-elking Slash 88 cattle, he lies! Which I've told him to his face."

Despite the quiet way in which he said it, here was a solid, blunt statement which simply could not be brushed aside with any expression of indignance. The shadow of an increasing uncertainty gripped Sherry.

"But — but fresh Slash 88 hides were found around the rancheria premises."

"If so, they'd been planted there," Carmack declared tersely. "Which is something else I've told Overton. Girl, let's give the Pomos credit for a little common sense. Had they really been slow-elking, would they deliberately advertise the fact by flaunting fresh, branded hides around? You know they wouldn't. All that hide talk was just an excuse to raid the Pomos and run them off their rancheria so it could be occupied."

Sherry showed a flash of earlier spirit. "But there's little about the rancheria strip to interest anyone who already owns the amount of range Kirby Overton does."

"It's not the land that concerns Mister Overton," retorted Carmack. "Its where it would put him. Right up against Long Seven. And last night he told me, flat out, that he intended to break me, run me out of this valley. There you have it, the real reason for the raid. So he could gain a foothold to go to work on me. As for him owning all he wants, you couldn't be further wrong. He's the sort who would never have enough of anything. With men like him, possession becomes a mania, whether it be for range, cattle, money — or power. And topping it all, he hates my immortal soul."

Vehemence deepened in Carmack. It pulled him to his feet and set him prowling up and down the room. Sherry watched him gravely. He swung an arm and made further harsh statement.

"I feel the same about him. It began the very first day we met, as kids in school. The moment we laid eyes on each other, we hated. We've hated ever since. Maybe it doesn't make much sense, but that's the way it's been, the way it is, and the way it will always be."

He came to a halt in front of Sherry and as he looked down at her, some of the harshness left him and he gave a short, apologetic laugh.

"Sorry to run on this way, but you wanted reasons and I've given you some."

Sherry drew a deep breath.

"Did Kirby Overton really make such a threat, Hugh? About breaking you and running you out of the valley?"

"He made it, all right."

"What did you tell him in return?"

"That I'd have considerable to say about any deal like that, myself."

It was Sherry's turn to shift restlessly. She struck her hands together a time or two in an unconscious gesture of uneasiness.

"I know you — and I know Kirby," she

said. "Hugh, this is something that must stop right now, before it grows really serious."

"It will turn just as serious as Overton wants to make it," Carmack said. "Which I've told him. And, girl, while you may know me, you don't know Kirby Overton. Nobody knows him, not thoroughly. All he ever shows is just what he wants seen. The rest is deep hidden unless you happen to catch him off guard or spur him past caution, like I managed to. And when you speak of things being serious, how about this? In the raid an old Pomo was ridden down. He was hurt so bad he died the next day."

Sherry came swiftly around. "I — I didn't know that. You're sure?"

"I'm sure."

She stood for a moment, biting a red underlip. She came closer to Carmack and looked up at him with a great soberness.

"Isn't there some way this thing can be patched up, Hugh?"

"Why not ask Overton that, Sherry. He's the one who is pushing on the rope."

"I will ask him. But now I'm asking you."

Carmack took another turn about the room.

"What would you have me do? Just step meekly aside — let him run me out of the valley? Not ever! For how about Kelly Logan? Half of everything that is Long Seven is hers. Any move Overton makes to hurt me, hurts little Kelly as well. And hurting her is something I don't take from anyone, regardless!"

Sherry struck her hands together again.

"Of course not; never anything like that. But maybe Kirby didn't really mean what he said. He could have spoken in thoughtless anger."

"He could have — but he didn't!" Carmack said, drily cynical. "That fellow, Sherry, would walk up and down the earth with ten foot strides and have everybody get out of his way."

"Perhaps if the Pomos were settled some place else, further out?" Sherry offered.

"No!"

Carmack laid the word down with a flat emphasis. He spun a cigarette into shape, lit it and inhaled deeply.

"No!" he repeated. "Understand, I'm not posing as being noble, or yet as my brother's keeper. But this is my valley as much as it is anybody's, for here I was born and here my folks lie buried, so I don't step aside one damn inch for anybody like Overton!"

He took another inhale, then went on slowly.

"Also, a man gets to have a feeling about a land he's lived on and ridden across through the years of his life. It becomes the one sure foundation of his days and nights, and in all its parts a familiar, comforting, well-loved world. As far back as I can remember, Bronco Charley and his Pomos have been such a part of my world. I intend to keep them so. I'm bringing them back to their rancheria, and if Overton — or anybody else — tries another raid, they'll have me to reckon with!"

Sherry moved to a window, stood looking out.

"I can understand your feelings, Hugh," she said carefully. "But aren't you being more idealistic than realistic? For the world does move, you know, and though you might like to, you can't be sure of keeping it to some exact pattern you happen to prefer."

"Maybe I can't," he admitted. "But I can stand up for my own rights and those of a few poor Pomo Indian devils who some would have us believe are not entitled to any rights at all."

Sherry faced him quickly, strong color flagging her cheeks.

"I never said I believed anything like that!"

"Of course you didn't," Carmack soothed. "I wasn't referring to you." The shadow of a smile relaxed the lines of his face. "We're being entirely too gloomy about this, borrowing trouble that may never come. Also, getting away from the reasons which brought me here, the main one of these, of course, being a chance to feast my eyes on you again. Then there was the question of some blankets, remember? Old ones you might be ready to throw away. From here I hit up Mrs. Cap McChesney, while Sam Hazle heads for the Lost Prairie country to see what luck he has with the Vinings and Nellis Coyne and at Jim Garland's. Between everybody, Sam and I figured we might rake up a dozen or fifteen."

Sherry wiped her hands on her apron and headed for an inner door.

"I have at least three for you. I'll get them."

When she returned, Carmack rolled the blankets into a tight bundle, carried them outside and tied them behind his saddle cantle. Sherry, following, watched with sober speculation. The crisp sunlight struck up rich gleams in her hair and tinted her cheeks, and she stood very fair in Carmack's eyes. As he went into his saddle she spoke quietly.

"That meat you gave the Pomos, Hugh — how long will it last them?"

"Quite a while. I beefed two critters."

"When they need more, you may slaughter one of ours."

He exclaimed quickly.

"Bless you! I may take you up on that, sometime. But the next beef for the Pomos will be Slash 88, whether Kirby Overton likes it or not. For he started this thing."

Down on Warrior Creek a rider hit the Gateway Ford at a run, foamed across and came spurring up the meadow. It was Sam Hazle. Sight of him and the obvious urgency with which he rode, brought Carmack high and alert in his saddle.

Sam hauled in, touched his hat to Sherry and gave Carmack the blunt word.

"They're tearing down the Pomo cabins!"

"Slash 88?" Carmack's voice rang.

"That's it."

"Overton there?"

"No," reported Sam, "but Furlong is, and feeling mighty damn biggity. I cut through the rancheria strip on my way to Lost Prairie and saw what was going on. I braced Furlong about it. He told me to keep right on traveling, which I did, seeing I didn't have a gun to match the one he was wearing. But," Sam added harshly, "from here I head home after the gun I didn't have, and then I'm riding down there again. And if

Mister Furlong wants to play hop-scotch I'll be happy to oblige. For that fellow never saw the day when he stood tall enough to run a blazer on me!"

Carmack nodded, his reaction bleak. "Just so. I'll be with you." He looked down. "Obliged for the blankets, Sherry. They'll be put to good use."

Before she could answer, he and Sam Hazle were racing away.

Sherry watched them out of sight, then turned slowly back to the house. From his chair, old Jeff Gailliard called.

"What the devil's all the hullabaloo about?"

Sherry told him, briefly and with reluctance, for because of his deepening infirmity and the morose viewpoint accompanying it, she had formed the habit of shielding him so far as she could from anything that might upset him. Now he snorted with dour impatience.

"What's a couple of Indian shanties? Pomos are just as well off in a brush wickiup, somewhere. Must be bigger things than that for folks to be concerned about, seems to me. Like, how stock are going to shape up through the hard winter ahead?"

"It could be an even harder winter for humans without a decent roof over their heads, Father," Sherry reminded him gently.

She left it that way, adjusting the blanket about his shoulders and moving the bench holding his can of pipe tobacco and block of sulphur matches a little closer to his hand.

Back in the kitchen she found she had little further interest in any baking, for she was possessed now of far too many disturbing thoughts. She had long known Hugh Carmack and Kirby Overton and had felt she knew them well. And though always fully aware of the strong current of dislike which lay between them, she had never believed it ran deeply enough to lead to such possibilities as now hovered darkly.

Again she struck her hands together, a characteristic gesture when upset or worried. In abrupt decision she hurried to her room and changed into riding clothes.

The rancheria was a mile wide strip of land with one end fronting on the west bank of Warrior Creek. Here the cabins of Bronco Charley and his Pomo people were scattered in a ragged line along a creek meadow. The structures had provided reasonable shelter to their former occupants, but even the best of them were little more than raw-boarded, ramshackle shanties, roughly thrown together. Which fact was serving Trace Furlong and three other Slash 88 riders in good stead. For it made the wrecking of the cabins not too difficult. The method used was fairly simple.

Ropes were noosed on rafter ends, then dallied about saddle horns and stout cow ponies put to the pull. Some solid wallops with an ax here and there would set rusty nails to squealing in protest. Shortly after, rafters would splinter, walls sag and finally collapse along with the shake roofs they had supported. Furlong's three helpers handled the ropes while he swung the ax.

Originally there had been a full two dozen cabins standing. Now a fourth of these lay in tangled ruin, with Furlong and his men hard at work on another. So caught up were they with destructive fever, Hugh Carmack rode to within thirty yards before Riff Powers, handling one of the ropes, became aware of his approach and called quick warning. The other two riders twisted in their saddles and Trace Furlong, ax in hand, stepped from the cabin door.

Sweat slimed his eye sockets and throat and darkly stained his shirt under his arms and across his chest. Sweat, mixed with dust, muddied his narrow cheeks. His eyes, as he faced Carmack, went flat and hard. He held silent, saying nothing.

Carmack wasted no time stating the issue.

"A big plenty of this, Furlong. Clear out — all of you!"

Furlong leaned his ax against a door post, scrubbed a shirt sleeve across his sweat-stung eyes, got out tobacco and papers and began rolling a cigarette. His narrowed glance noted that Carmack, who generally rode without a gun, now had one holstered at his belt, and also a Winchester slung in a saddle boot. However, the odds were top heavy at four to one and as Furlong licked his cigarette into shape he tipped his head, his glance reaching right and left, swiftly touching his men. They got the message and swung to face Carmack fully. Furlong lit his cigarette and spoke thin taunt through the smoke.

"Maybe we don't intend to clear out. What then?"

"Then we argue!" Carmack rocked a little forward in his saddle.

"This is between Slash 88 and those damned thieving Pomos," Furlong protested. "It's none of your affair."

Carmack was implacable. "You listened in last night when I gave Kirby Overton the word — which was to keep off this property. I meant it then, I mean it now. Get off this land!"

Trace Furlong took a deep drag on his cigarette, then flicked the butt on the ground in front of Carmack's horse in a gesture of defiance.

"No! We're staying!"

"Proud at four to one, eh?" Carmack murmured sarcastically. "I'd think on it if I were you. Things may not be what they seem."

Wariness touched Furlong. He stared at Carmack, black eyes narrowed and searching. He swung his head, glancing right and left. But the bulk of the cabin hid the creek from him and it was from this point that Sam Hazle quietly approached, to swing his horse abruptly past the cabin corner. He grinned sardonically at the startled Slash 88 riding boss.

"Back like I promised. With a gun. Want to try your luck?"

Under the sweat and dust, Furlong's dark face became a stone cold, expressionless mask. The odds had been cut in half. For the moment he could think of nothing to say, but one of his men exclaimed nervously.

"Hell! They're all around us. Look yonder!"

Now it was Marty McGah who came riding, first at a leisurely jog, then, nearing these men and reading the strain in their attitudes, at a short, swift run to come quickly up beside Carmack.

Most generally, Marty's long, good natured face reflected an impudent half-grin, as though the world and all in it furnished him with a never ending fund of inner amusement. Now, however, with the ominous signs all here and easy to read, he showed sober concern.

"Would it be any of my business what this is all about?" he asked, drawling.

Carmack waved an indicating arm.

"There it is. These brave lads were working up a real sweat — tearing down cabins. I just told them I didn't like the idea."

The work of destruction had been going on near the head of the meadow and Marty, coming up from the lower end, now had his first glimpse of the tumbled, splintered ruins. He had a good look, a long one, and his face tightened. Of a sudden there was no quirk of humor in him anywhere. Over the space of a long breath, Marty McGah became an angry man. There was bright challenge in the glance he laid on Furlong.

"Overton's orders, or your own idea?"

Furlong shrugged, made no reply.

"Then I only know what I see," Marty said. "And what I see I like no better than does Carmack. I suggest, Furlong, that you get the hell out of here!"

Trace Furlong was no coward, being as ready as any to face up to violence if such was really warranted and there was no other solution. However, behind his pose of remote arrogance and contempt, he was a careful and a scheming man. His orders from Kirby Overton had been to wreck the Pomo cabins, which could have presupposed a readiness to make an all-out fight over the issue, should matters reach that critical a point. And here, it seemed, they had.

But though perfectly willing to stand up for his hire, with gunsmoke if necessary, the careful streak in Furlong suggested he wait until Kirby Overton proved by act, as well as with words, that he was ready to face the smoke, too. Because, once long ago, Trace Furlong had gone far out on a limb for another man and found himself left hanging there. It provided a lesson he'd never forgotten.

When Sam Hazle, without a gun, had shown earlier, it had pleased the contempt and arrogance in Furlong to roughly order old Sam on his way. But Sam was back now, and armed, grinning like a grizzled old wolf, ready to leap and snap. And there was Hugh Carmack chilly of eye and ready for anything. And Marty McGah, openly siding with Carmack. Whatever the odds had been once, they meant nothing now.

It galled Furlong deeply to admit it, even to himself. But at this particular moment, retreat loomed as the only intelligent move. Plenty of time later, he reasoned swiftly, to meet the challenge and make the fight if that was the way it would have to be.

He turned to his men, his words thin and curt.

"Roll your ropes. We're moving out."

The three other Slash 88 riders did not argue. If Furlong wanted no trouble, certainly they didn't.

Furlong picked up his ax and walked over to his horse. He sheathed the ax in some folds of leather and tied it behind his saddle. He stepped astride and swung his horse to face Carmack, as though he was about to say something, for his tight lips writhed a trifle. But he held back vocal utterance and let his eyes say it all. They glittered with a dark and remembering venom.

He spun his horse and led the way out of the meadow at a run.

Carmack turned to Marty McGah. "My friend, you showed up at a very handy time."

"Pure chance," shrugged Marty. "I was just riding and looking." He stared soberly after the departing Slash 88 contingent, then had another look at the ruined cabins. He shook a rueful head. "Overton must be out of his mind, dishing up destruction and misery like this. I've a mind to drop in on that fellow and have me a real shoulder to shoulder talk. Maybe I can knock some sense into him."

"Not a chance," Carmack declared. "This is the beginning of something he's had in mind for a long, long time — and he's got his neck bowed. So you'd just be wasting your time. It's my feeling this is one of those things that must get a lot worse before it will get better. Which is not a good, or comfortable feeling by any hell of a ways. But it is the feeling I got. So I'm going to be guided accordingly!"

5

To those who claimed it as their world, the valley of Warrior Creek was a land of two parts, east side and west side, the creek being the dividing line. A man was either a west-sider or an east-sider, the designation being purely one of location, however, with no deeper interpretation or meaning.

From north to south, east siders were Jeff Gailliard, Captain Rufus McChesney, Marty

McGah and Nellis Coyne. West side, north to south, it ran Hugh Carmack's Long Seven, then the rancheria strip, then Kirby Overton's Slash 88, biggest outfit in the area, and finally Cal Vining and Jim Garland well to the south, controlling between them the best of the Lost Prairie range. Town stood on the west side of the creek and fairly central in the valley.

Like the outfit it was the heart of, Slash 88 headquarters was large and imposing. The original and rather humble headquarters, which had been the home of his father and mother, and in which he had been born, Kirby Overton had caused to be torn down to make room for the present one. The new ranchhouse was a big, blocky, two-storied affair and stood out in white painted eminence as if it would assert an over-all and somewhat arrogant authority.

In a land pledged pretty much to the basic, practical fundamentals of living, the new Slash 88 ranchhouse, with its imposing size, caused considerable speculation as to why any man, especially a single one like Kirby Overton, would want to build such a home. Various ideas had been voiced, with pungent, sarcastic old Sam Hazle coming up with one that stopped all others.

"Preparing for the day when he'll be

God," was the way Sam put it.

Sherry Gailliard had heard of Sam Hazle's statement and it came back to her now as she crossed the creek at Middle Ford and saw the Slash 88 ranchhouse lifting out there ahead. Sunlight laid a bright glitter on the white painted walls and made the building stand out in strong focus against a more subdued background.

There was no stir of life about the place until Sherry reined to a stop below the steps at one end of the long, galleried porch. Then it was Kirby Overton who stepped from a door and came to greet her. At the moment he was without a coat, but his shirt was fresh and white, his string tie in place and a cigar was burning between his teeth. His clean shaven cheeks were ruddy, his hair neatly combed. He made a strong, aggressive looking figure. As Sherry dismounted he dropped down the steps, smiling.

"Well — surprise. And a welcome one!"

Sherry faced him soberly.

"Don't be too sure, Kirby. Better wait until you've heard what I have to say."

Overton's heartiness shaded off slightly.

"Your father? Something wrong — ?"

"Father's no different than usual," Sherry broke in, drawing off her gloves. "This has to do with, well —," she drew a deep breath and took the plunge — "the thing that is rising between you and Hugh Carmack. And it must not go any further, Kirby."

Overton's lips tightened about his cigar.

"I thought we'd about settled that on the way home from the dance last night."

"Last night I did not fully realize how serious it was," Sherry said simply. "And I know things now that I did not know then."

"Such as?"

"Your men tearing down Pomo cabins on the rancheria strip. Did you order that?"

Overton was silent for a moment. Then he rolled his cigar to the other corner of his mouth and jerked a beckoning head.

"Come on into the office, where we can thrash this thing out in comfort."

Sherry went along with him to the door he'd emerged from. This let them into a fairly large room containing half a dozen chairs and a big, heavy oak center table, on which were spread several account books. Evidently Overton had been at work here when she rode up.

There was a rack on an inner wall holding three rifles and a pair of shotguns, one of these a sawed-off weapon. Two Colt guns hung on pegs beside the rack, one in a shoulder holster harness, the other swung to a regular cartridge belt. Backed up in one corner was a ceiling-tall, oak cabinet with a solid door held closed by hasp and padlock.

Overton swung a chair around for Sherry and dropped into the one across the table from her. He took a deep drag at his cigar, then held it in front of him and stared at the gray-ashed tip. He spoke slowly.

"Now about the Pomo cabins —."

"Yes," Sherry said. "You ordered that?"

He shrugged slightly. "I ordered it."

"Why?"

"For the same reason I had the Pomos run off the land in the first place. To put a stop to the slow-elking of my cattle. If the cabins were left standing, the Pomos would come sneaking back. This way they'll clear out, once and for all."

"You feel you have the right to treat them so?" Sherry's glance was intent.

Overton reared back in his chair, shrugged again.

"I've the right to take any measures necessary to protect my property. When I stop slow-elking, I'm doing just that."

She studied him with the same sober gravity she had met him with. Here was a directness of statement almost convincing. Yet, not over an hour gone, Hugh Carmack had declared things so differently.

"I've heard the slow-elking charge denied, Kirby."

"By Carmack, I suppose?"

"Yes."

"He would!" Overton showed the beginnings of harshness. "It's his word against mine. Naturally he'd try and make me out a liar. Would you, too?"

Quick color filled Sherry's cheeks and her eyes flashed. But she kept her words even and quiet.

"I'm trying to find out the real truth, that's all. And to head off this senseless animosity between you and Hugh Carmack. Tell me, Kirby — what are your real intentions toward Hugh?"

Watching carefully, Sherry saw this man across the table begin to retreat within himself, saw a shield of wariness glaze his eyes.

"By that — meaning what?" he asked.

"That you'd like to break him — run him out of the valley."

Overton hesitated, then nodded.

"I hold no brief for Carmack, or liking, either, which you well know. Bluntly, I hate him — just as he hates me. The man insists on cluttering up the trail. Sometimes I think it's fated that one or the other of us has to go. And I intend to make sure it isn't me. If Carmack wants no trouble, all he has to do is keep out of my way!"

"What is your way, Kirby?"

In growing irritation before the insistent pressure of Sherry's questioning, Overton waved his cigar in a short, curt arc.

"My way? Why to get ahead, of course. To build, grow — expand. Certainly not to hold back, hanging on to a lot of outdated sentiment. Which seems to satisfy Carmack. Well, it doesn't satisfy me, and if he tries to block me, then — !" Overton waved his cigar again.

"How, as you put it, is Hugh trying to block you?"

"For one thing, he'd throw his weight around over this Pomo affair. And just where does he get the idea it's any business of his?"

"Perhaps he feels they're being treated unfairly. Hugh's the sort to take the side of the under-dog."

"Maybe," said Overton, his lip curling slightly, "you feel the same as he does."

"That could be. And don't get sarcastic with me, Kirby!" Again there was a flare of spirit in Sherry's eyes.

He recognized the danger signals. "Sorry. Didn't mean to be. But all this fuss over something of so little account, gets me edgy."

"That's just it," corrected Sherry, "it isn't of little account. Murder is never of little account."

"Murder!" Overton stared. "What do you mean — murder?"

"During the raid," Sherry said carefully, "one of your men rode down a Pomo old one, injuring him so bad he died the next day. A court of law might call that murder, Kirby."

"I know nothing of any Pomo being hurt and dying," Overton declared. "What proof have you such a thing happened?"

"I've Hugh Carmack's word for it."

"And where did he get his information?"

For this, Sherry had no answer. She faltered slightly in admitting it. "I — I don't know. He must have heard of it somewhere."

"Hearing is cheap, anytime," Overton said bluntly. "Carmack certainly wasn't on hand during the raid, so all he could know about it is what he's been told. And who by? Most probably by the Pomos themselves. And who can lie faster? Naturally they'd put up all manner of wild claims, trying to win sympathy. They lied about the slow-elking, why wouldn't they lie about everything else?"

Sherry went through her usual move of striking her hands together a time or two when upset and uncertain.

"I don't know," she said wearily. "No, I don't know about that. But I do know I want this — this senseless animosity between you and Hugh stopped before it leads to anything worse. I've told Hugh that and I'm telling you the same. And it can be stopped if you'll both just be content to live and let live."

Overton observed her carefully.

"If it should come to a showdown, which side will you be on, Sherry — Carmack's or mine?"

Instantly Sherry was flaring again.

"What an idiotic question! I'll be inclined to hate you both as fools!"

Overton shook his head, showing a faint, mirthless smile.

"Not both of us, my dear. For if you hate the fool, it will be Carmack, not me. For he'll be the one who really starts it. His kind are the ones who always start things in this world. Because they're so damned self-righteous. They're the ones who burn the witches, crucify the innocent. They —."

Overton broke off, his head tipped as he listened.

Now Sherry heard it, too. The thump of

running hoofs, fast approaching.

Overton got to his feet, went to the door and had his look, then stepped quickly along the porch. Sherry followed him.

Pulling in and leaving their saddles over at the corrals were Trace Furlong and three other riders. As his heels hit the ground, Furlong rapped an order, then turned and came across the interval to the ranchhouse.

Furlong's face was dark and full of tight anger as he topped the porch steps. He looked along past Overton at Sherry Gailliard with an insolent appraisal that brought the hot blood to her cheeks. It was always so with this man Furlong, she thought furiously. Every look he had ever thrown her way had been an insult.

"You're back a little quick, Trace," Overton said with a rising inflection. "Why?"

"Carmack!" Furlong spat the word in his high, hard tone. "Him and Hazle and McGah. They run us out."

"And you stood for it?" There was the crackle of a swift anger in the question.

Furlong's shrug was sullen. "My orders didn't reach any further than tearing down the damned shanties."

"Did those fellows have guns?"

"Carmack and Hazle did. McGah might have had one in his pocket. You never know about that wild Irishman."

"You had guns, didn't you?" Overton charged. "You and Powers and the other two? And the odds were with you, four to three. Why did you back down?"

"I told you," Furlong blurted. "My orders were to flatten the shanties. Nothing was said about getting into a shoot-out over them."

Overton kept his back to Sherry while he sorted out his feelings and strove to get them under control. A curt nod and equally curt, "All right!" dismissed Trace Furlong for the moment, sending him back to where the other three riders waited by the corrals. When he finally came around, Overton's face was stiffly impassive, but he could not fully hide the smoldering anger that congested his eyes.

"You see," he said, his words brittle. "It's like I said. Carmack is bound to set up trouble. He just can't leave well enough alone."

Sherry began pulling on her gloves.

"That won't do, Kirby," she said quietly.

"What won't do?"

"Attempting to justify your own actions by blaming someone else for theirs. Particularly when you are in the wrong. Because Hugh Carmack is more justified in objecting to mistreatment of the Pomos than you are in inflicting it. After all, there is such a thing as right in the world."

The smoldering gleam in Overton's eyes deepened.

"Would you be taking sides?"

"If so," Sherry retorted, "it is on the side of my conscience." She moved toward the steps.

Overton caught at her arm.

"No — don't go! There mustn't be any quarrel between you and me, Sherry. I'm sorry if I spoke roughly. It's just — well, hard for me to hold in when everywhere I turn, there's Carmack in my way. All my life it seems it's been so, and I just can't help but — !" He broke off, shaking his head, biting back some words, then quickly replacing them with more placating ones. "Don't go," he said again. "We can talk this all out."

Sherry studied him for a discerning moment. "There is no need our trying to talk anything out unless you are willing to drop this blind animosity toward Hugh Carmack. Also," she added, pulling her arm free, "to stop striking at defenseless folk like the Pomos."

Overton swung his shoulders, clenching and unclenching his hands, restless with banked up feeling.

"That isn't as easy as it sounds," he said a little thickly. "I mean about Carmack. For hate is like any of the other deeper emotions. When you've known it all your life you just can't throw it aside at a moment's notice. No, Sherry — it's not that simple. And the Pomos — would you have me sit back and do nothing about it while those damned Indians steal me blind?"

"That's nonsense," Sherry said crisply. "The Pomos couldn't possibly be hurting you that bad. For that matter I'm not at all convinced they ever stole or slow-elked a single head of your cattle. Neither am I convinced that Hugh Carmack is getting in your way any more than you are getting in his. But there are one or two things that I do know. You ordered the raid on the Pomos and you ordered their cabins torn down. Also, you were furious just now because your men did not make a shooting affair of it when Hugh Carmack made them stop any further destruction. Kirby, I'm no child. Don't try and convince me that black is white."

"Then it's Carmack you believe." Overton could no longer hold back his rising anger. "He's poisoned you against me."

"Nobody has poisoned me against anyone," Sherry said, dropping down the steps. "But I have to trust and believe in logic and my own common sense."

She reached her horse and went into the saddle. From there, gravely still, she considered Overton once more, regret in her glance.

"I'm sorry, Kirby. But I'm afraid you just can't understand that there are greater values in life than dollars and possessions."

She spun her horse and loped away, knowing that Overton's angry glance was following her, yet far more conscious of the calculating, insulting stare of the man who now stood in the doorway of the ranch bunkhouse, Trace Furlong.

Kirby Overton watched Sherry Gailliard ride down to the Middle Ford, splash across it and move from sight beyond the willow and alder thickets which lined the creek. He tried his cigar, found it dead and soggy and threw it aside with a hard gesture. He lifted a harsh call.

"Furlong!"

He turned back into the office and got a fresh cigar. He had clipped the end from this and was lighting up when Trace Furlong stepped into the room. The Slash 88 riding boss dragged up a chair, settled into it and began building a cigarette.

Overton looked down at him, florid cheeks and pale eyes hectic with feeling.

"You had the odds on Carmack. Why didn't you go after him?"

Furlong shrugged. "Like I said. My orders didn't say anything about getting into a shootout. When they do, then I want to be damned sure that the man who gives me the orders is right in there with me."

Overton's eyes squeezed down slightly.

"Just what in hell does that mean?"

"Why now," Furlong said, "once when I was young and very foolish, I stepped out into the middle of a street for a boss. But he backed out of the party and left me out in that wide, wide street all by myself. That's learning a lesson the hard way, which I did, and it's stayed with me ever since."

"You think I'd leave you hanging?" charged Overton.

Furlong touched a match to his cigarette, relished a deep inhale.

"Didn't say you would. Just saying I want to be sure you wouldn't."

"You could be losing your nerve." There was the faintest hint of a sneer in Overton's words.

Furlong challenged him instantly.

"You think so, then you'd best write out my time!"

Overton swung back and forth across the room coming to an angry stop.

"Sorry. And I don't think so. But having Carmack block me again like this, turns me inside out!"

"Sure," said Furlong, mollified by the apology. "I know how you feel. You think I enjoyed being told to get the hell off the rancheria strip? I don't like being pushed around any more than the next."

"Could Carmack have been bluffing, do you think?"

Furlong shook his head. "He wasn't bluffing. He was cocked and ready for anything. So you better make your mind up, one way or another."

"On what?" Overton stared through a cloud of pale cigar smoke.

"Either that you do or you don't. Either you take off the gloves, prepared to go all the way, or you pull in your horns and don't try and go anywhere."

"What in hell do you think I'm doing?" Overton demanded hotly. "Why do you think I ordered the raid? Why — ?"

"I know — I know," Furlong broke in. "Just the same, you're made, you're set to do two things. First is to bust Carmack, still circling the edges, hoping Carmack will drop dead, maybe. Which he's hardly liable to. According to talk your Second is to move through the hole that would make and take over everything you can in the valley and run things to suit yourself. But you can't do the last until you've handled the first chore. Which won't be noways easy. For when you set out to take care of Carmack you better be prepared to carry through, right down to the last load in your gun. Because that's the way he'll feel about his side of the argument."

"You think I'm afraid of him?"

Furlong considered a moment, then shook his head.

"No, not man to man. But I do think you're a little leary of the reaction that could come from other sources. Carmack's got his share of friends. You got to be prepared to look them in the eye, too."

"If you're asking me to do something, what is it?"

"I'm not asking you to do anything," Furlong shrugged. "I'm just trying to find out, once and for all, how many blue chips you're willing to throw into the game."

Overton's jaw tightened. "I didn't come this far to start backing up. I'm going to get what I want!"

"Keno! Then let's take the gloves off before we run out of time. How do we really start in on Carmack?"

Overton rolled his cigar across his lips and calculated for a moment.

"He's set to make issue over the rancheria strip. So that's how it will be. We'll make a gather and start drifting in some cattle. When Carmack starts moving them off again, which he's almost certain to, then he's monkeying with another man's cattle on neutral government ground, and that leaves him liable to whatever comes his way. In the mean time, put a man out there to keep an eye on things. Tell him to keep out of sight and report back any activity by Long Seven."

"Most of the shanties are still standing," pointed out Furlong. "How about them?"

"They'll keep. We can always take care of them, later."

Furlong got to his feet and moved to the door. He paused there and dipped his head toward the guns hanging on the inner wall.

"Those just ornaments, or do you figure to carry one?"

"I'll carry one," Overton told him curtly. "I'll use it, too, any time the need arises!"

6

The day was nearly run when Hugh Carmack and Sam Hazle got back to Long Seven headquarters. In the fast fading afternoon light a ground reined saddle mount crowded the cavvy corral fence and dozed on three legs. Carmack recognized the animal and looked around for its owner. He saw her coming past the corner of the cookshack, hand in hand with Kelly Logan, who was half-walking, half-skipping while relating some childish episode in her eager, breathless way.

Carmack dismounted and Sherry Gailliard, meeting his glance, showed a small, shadowed smile.

"Kelly and I," she said, "have had quite a visit. We've played with the pet chipmunks and been down to the pasture to see Pepper. And Benjy Todd, by promising to make some dried apple pie, has bribed me into staying for supper."

"For which," applauded Carmack, "I may give him a raise in wages."

"You had good luck in your quest for blankets?"

"The best," Carmack nodded. "All collected and delivered."

He turned to unsaddle his horse, but

Sam Hazle waved him off. "I'll take care of it."

Carmack slid an arm about Kelly's small shoulders.

"Case and Neal get in from town?"

Kelly shook her head. "Not yet."

"A pair of scoundrels," Carmack said. "Making the most of the weekend. Well, they earned the right."

The sun fell into a cauldron of exploding scarlet and old rose and twilight hurried down out of the hills. Benjy Todd lit the cookshack lamps and supper was eaten in a room full of cheer and warmth amid the savory steams and fragrances lifted from Benjy's stove. With feminine company on hand, Benjy outdid himself, scuttling busily back and forth, in particular fussing over Kelly.

"Like a biddy with one chick," Carmack told Sherry in a low toned, smiling aside. "Kelly bosses him scandalously and winds him around her little finger. But she dotes on him."

What with being up late the night before, followed by an active day of getting re-acquainted with the ranch, Kelly was beginning to nod by the time the meal was finished. She announced her intention of going to bed, then shyly asked Sherry if she'd like to tuck her in.

Sherry looked at Carmack. "May I?"

"Of course."

He went ahead to the ranchhouse, lit a couple of lamps. He looked around with some discomfiture. The house was not littered, particularly, but six weeks without active occupancy had peopled the rooms with the usual number of dusty ghosts. Somewhat lamely he began to apologize, but Sherry stopped him.

"It's home, isn't it? And there's nothing wrong that a little more regular living with wouldn't cure."

"Maybe," Carmack said swiftly, "I might interest you there?"

Sherry flushed, tossing her head.

"That, sir, is taking unfair advantage of a woman's natural instinct for tidiness. Besides suggesting something I'd have to think about for a long, long time."

Carmack bent his tall length for Kelly's goodnight kiss, then watched the two of them go along to Kelly's room, moving in the bright bloom of light from the lamp Sherry carried.

He was standing in grave thought over a cigarette when Sherry came back to the living room and set her lamp on the table.

"Now I'll have to be getting along home,

for Dad and the men will worry," she said. "But first I've a few things to tell you. Before I came here, I rode in at Slash 88. I saw Kirby Overton and asked him the same thing I asked you, Hugh. That he drop his side of this blind antagonistic stand-off between you two."

"Interesting," Carmack drawled. "What did he say?"

"Several things. Mainly, I'm afraid, reasons for not doing what I asked."

Carmack bobbed his head.

"Which I would expect. This thing is written, Sherry. It's in the book. And the more I think on it the more certain I am that it is going to take something considerably stronger than words to settle it."

"Which doesn't dismay you?"

He considered this, lips pursed while he stared straight ahead.

"Dismay isn't the right word," he said presently. "While I regret the necessity of it, the fact itself doesn't dismay me. If it did, it would mean I was afraid of Overton. Which I'm not." He swung his glance to touch her. "What did you say to him when he refused to do as you wished."

"I told him both he and you were idiots," Sherry answered with feeling.

Carmack chuckled. "Now that could very

well be. And with the whole thing not worth bothering your head over."

"I didn't say that. Of course I'm bothered about it. How could I be otherwise? Oh, Hugh — isn't there something — some way — ?"

"Sorry, but I'm afraid not. Let's just consider the youngster you tucked in a minute ago," he reminded. "As I've told you before, should I give way to Overton I'd be letting Kelly down as well as myself. And that I can't, and won't, do!"

"I know," Sherry admitted, "I know! But while I was at Slash 88, Trace Furlong and three others rode in. I heard what Furlong had to report. That you and Sam Hazle and Marty McGah had stopped further destruction of the Pomo cabins — and how you did it."

"Ha!" Carmack exclaimed. "And did friend Kirby like the news?"

"He was furious." Sherry stirred in restless worry. "He gave Furlong fits for not standing up to you, even if it had meant gun-play, shooting!" She broke off, big eyed and taut in the realization of what this could mean. Somewhat lamely she went on. "Here I am, carrying tales between two men I've known and liked all my life. I feel like some sort of traitor, an informer."

"Nonsense!" scoffed Carmack. "You're just a thoroughly sound person, refusing to compromise your sense of what is right."

She struck her hands together in her peculiar little gesture.

"If I could only be completely sure — !"

"You're sure," Carmack told her. "You're absolutely sure. But because you've known the man for so long and have found some pleasure in his company, you're seeking a way to excuse him. And there is no way to excuse piracy."

"Yet only last night," Sherry whispered, as if repeating a thought to herself, "I went to a dance with him."

"In a thing of this sort," Carmack observed gently, "you hear what you hear, you see what you see, and then you know what you know. Out of it all you form a judgement. So long as it is an honest judgement — and with you I know it would have to be — then nothing else counts."

Sherry mused soberly a little time, then nodded. "That is a comforting way of putting it. And now I must go."

Abruptly she was brisk, moving to leave.

"I'm riding home with you," Carmack said.

She protested mildly. "It isn't necessary, Hugh."

"Perhaps not necessary," he declared. "But pleasurable for me at least. It's been a long time since we've ridden together. Too long."

They rode across an earth deep stained with night's black mystery. Stars arched overhead in a vast, cold glitter, and behind them winter lay, waiting its turn to move in. Already its slicing breath was in the slow-stirring air.

They came to the Gateway Ford and splashed through and a touch of spray, whipped up by the hoofs of her horse, struck Sherry's cheeks and made her gasp.

"Winter!" she said. "I hate to see it on the way. It is the cruel season, Hugh."

"Yes," he agreed. "Particularly if you've no decent roof over your head, or a fire to sit beside, or food to put in your stomach. Wonder if Kirby Overton thought of that when he started in on the Pomos?"

She had no answer for him until they had crossed the meadow and climbed the little slope to Gateway headquarters. Then:

"There's a relentless streak in you, Hugh Carmack."

"I don't know about the relentless part, but when I figure I'm right I try and hang on," he admitted.

A figure drifted up through the dark and

Orde Dardin's murmur was faintly admonitory.

"About set to go looking for you, young lady."

Sherry was contrite. "Sorry, Orde. I shouldn't have stayed so late. Father has been worrying, of course?"

"Some," Orde said, taking her rein.

Sherry dropped quickly from her saddle. "Thanks for everything, Hugh. I — I think you're right, too."

She was gone, then, hurrying to the ranch-house and stepping through a door which let out a brief interval of rectangular light as it opened and closed.

"All my fault," Hugh Carmack told Orde Dardin. "Maybe some was Benjy Todd's. Between us we got Sherry to stay to supper."

"Glad you did," said Dardin. "Old Jeff, he grumbles considerable when she's away, but he can't expect her at his side all the time. She's been mighty faithful, and has a right to get off for a few hours now and then. What's the latest on Overton?"

Carmack briefly sketched the day's happenings, and the Gateway foreman, as he worked at unsaddling Sherry's horse, swore softly.

"It's finally beginning to show," he declared. "Overton's real makeup, I mean. Somehow I never did cotton to that man. Those damn pale eyes of his — they're all surface, somehow — hard surface that you can't see past. And me, I figure that a bad eye in a human means the same thing that it does in any four-legged critter; they just ain't to be trusted. That feller could be shaking up a lot of trouble for himself, Hugh."

"Depends on how far he tries to reach," Carmack said. "Could be, realizing now that several of us don't exactly see eye to eye with him, he'll back off and behave himself."

"Not him," differed Orde Dardin emphatically. "No, sir — not Kirby Overton. His kind never quits trying to claw the other fellow down. He's the sort just bound to be big as hell, even if it kills him!"

In Sadie Colo's relatively bright eighteen years of existence there had been few highlights. Orphaned while very young, she could not remember her parents and had managed to exist only because of the willing, though too often scanty bounty of others of the tribe. She had early learned the place of the squaw in the world of the Pomo Indian. So she had toiled as her sisters had toiled. She had gathered and carried endless amounts of firewood, dug and bleached camas root, and in seasons of shortest fare had trudged many a weary mile in quest of piñon nuts. All such tasks she had known while still a silent, brown-faced girl, stoically accepting them as an integral part of her world.

Personal belongings were few. Of these, most treasured was a dress given her by an older squaw who had grown out of it. It was of calico and was worn and faded, but once its colors of red and green had been bright and gay, and it was Sadie Colo's dearest possession.

At the moment, however, the dress was not here in this brush camp under the shadow of Midnight Butte. Instead, during the confusion and fear and anger of the raid that drove the Pomos from their cabin homes, the dress was left behind. And Sadie Colo had mourned for it ever since.

Now, as she lay in her corner of a brush wickiup and stared up at the cold star gleam leaking through the loose brush roof overhead, she made up her mind about the dress. Tomorrow she would go after it. Tomorrow, on the pretense of searching for camas root, she would get well apart from everyone, then head for the rancheria strip. That it was miles distant did not dissuade her. Only the dress counted.

By mid-morning next day she was on her way, trudging along as fast as her short sturdiness would allow. With each swinging step she toed in slightly, yet moving with a sure lightness that was heritage of ten thousand wild ancestors. Also, with an instinctive wariness, she used every natural advantage for concealment.

She had crossed Long Seven range a full mile west of the headquarters, and when she left Long Seven ground she was on the rancheria strip, where she turned east to Warrior Creek and its long-running meadows where stood the rightful cabins of her people.

These she approached with extreme caution, and while she saw that some of the cabins had been demolished, she knew relief over the fact that the one she had called home was still standing. At the same time, in her young, inarticulate way, she felt a smoldering anger over the destruction of the others.

For the best part of half an hour she crouched at the edge of the meadow, watching, listening. Nothing moved and a big silence held the world, broken only by the faint murmur of the creek waters and the even fainter clarion of a high-flying wedge of honker geese, winging south. Convinced finally that she had the meadow to herself, she scurried across to the cabins.

The door of the one she sought was open and she ducked quickly inside. No mischief had been done in this cabin, for here was only the confusion of a hurried leaving at the time of the raid. The treasured dress was exactly as she had left it, hung carefully in a corner. She lifted it down, her black, doe-soft eyes shining her pleasure. She held it up and admired it and pressed a brown cheek against its worn and faded fabric.

She gave herself little time to exult, for it was a long way back to the Midnight Butte camp. However, now that she was about it, she would take back some other things besides the dress. She stripped a tattered blanket from a bunk, spread it on the floor and began making up a pack, the first item of which was the dress, carefully folded. To this she added all that was handy which she figured would be of use.

She had just built her pack into a thick bundle when a sound at the door brought her swiftly around. Her breath caught in her throat in a tight, silent little cry. She was looking up at a man's hulking figure. . . .

When Trace Furlong, as directed by Kirby Overton, ordered Hobey Beecham to the rancheria strip to keep an eye on things, the order was acknowledged with no particular grace. For Beecham was still physically sore and stiff from the brief, but violent going over he'd taken at the hands of Hugh Carmack in Russ Herrick's Acme Bar. In addition to his physical misery, Beecham was also sore in his mind over the fact that after he had stepped forth to mix it with Carmack, no one from Slash 88, including Kirby Overton himself, had done anything of account in backing him up. He had been left alone to take the rough brunt of things, and the fact still rankled.

So, from Slash 88 it was a sullen Hobey Beecham who cut back to town after a bottle to keep him company while he lay around at the rancheria. And shortly after Beecham left town with his bottle, Packy Devine also rode out.

The Monday morning ride was a regular ritual with Packy Devine, for Monday was the slack day of the week where business was concerned and in his younger days Packy had been a jockey, and the love of a good horse under him had never left him.

He had such a mount in his stable, a chestnut filly with a good strain of warm blood in her. She was spirited, sensitive to proper treatment and was Packy's particular pride and joy. Any other animal in his stable or corral he would rent or sell or trade if the price or deal was right. But no one other than himself ever rode the filly, and she was not for sale or trade at any price or under any condition.

Both rider and mount rejoiced in the action and freedom of these rides. Packy always kept strictly to the creek meadows, for here the ground was level, springy and reliable underfoot, and here, from time to time along certain stretches he would let the filly really run, while he, up on a light copy of the McClellan saddle, would regain some faint flavor of the great days of his youth when he had lifted many a thoroughbred home ahead of the speeding pack while the thunder of the crowd built its great, overhanging echo.

Packy had seen Hobey Beecham ride in and out of town. He had seen Beecham with his bottle, taking a drag from it even while riding, and at this Packy's lip had curled in disgust. For while he liked a drink himself, now and then, Packy had small patience with those who went off by themselves for a bout with a bottle. Somehow, as he saw it, this suggested an inner tawdriness and weakness that just didn't fit in with his own spunky attitude toward life. For that matter, he'd never had any use for Hobey Beecham.

Now, as he rode the creek meadows northward, Packy marked the fresh tracks of Beecham's horse ahead of him, and having no desire to overhaul the man and suffer the necessity of having to talk to someone he heartily disliked, he held the eager filly back, figuring Beecham would presently take the turn-off to Slash 88 at Middle Ford. Instead, Beecham kept on to the rancheria strip.

Here, with the contents of his bottle considerably lowered, and having reined in to take another drink, Beecham held off and stared, not entirely sure he'd actually seen what he thought he had. Out there the stocky, but not ungraceful figure of a young Pomo squaw had just hurried across the meadow and into one of the cabins.

For a little time Beecham stayed as he was, looking carefully around. He had helped in the raid on the Pomos, and while they were considered to be a docile and somewhat spiritless people, he now reasoned with a half-drunken cunning that a man could never be too sure. Besides that pretty little squaw, some of the other Indians might be close and feeling hostile.

Presently, with renewed confidence, Beecham rode deeper into the meadow, there to leave his horse and sneak cautiously the balance of the way on foot. He wanted to get his hands on that little squaw before she could run or yell. He was sure now that he knew which one she was. He had seen her before at various times and had marked her youthful prettiness. So now, as he moved through the cabin door and saw her there before him, he became all animal.

He stood, staring at her, swaying from side to side in a drunken looseness while a primitive terror lifted Sadie Colo from her knees beside her bundle and started her backing away. But this single roomed cabin was small and she had little room to maneuver in. Hobey Beecham, lips loose and lecherous, prowled after her.

She could smell the whiskey reek on him, could see that he was partially drunk, and so knew a thread of hope that she might dodge past him and gain the open door. But despite his wavering, lurching advance, he was too fast for her, and when he finally had her fully cornered and she made her desperate try to get past him, he lunged in front of her and caught her.

She was young, she was strong and savagely frightened, and she fought him with all the silent fury and tenacity of a wildcat. Gallant as her effort was, his bulk and strength were too much for her. He began forcing her back and down. She got a hand free and clawed at his face, aiming for his eyes. She did not quite reach these, but she did scar him again and again from cheekbone to chin, raking bloody furrows with her slicing nails.

In fighting down her first struggles, Beecham had merely leered at her efforts to break free. But now the pain of those clawing, gouging nails turned loose a brutal anger and his leer became a snarl and he cursed her and hit her in the face with a pounding fist. Then he locked fingers about her throat.

Sadie Colo's world went away from her in choking, pain riven madness.

From behind a screen of creek alders, with the chestnut filly standing quiet under him, Packy Devine wondered at the significance of a close-coupled grullo saddle mount, ground-reined out there in the meadow below the Pomo cabins. Packy recognized the horse at a glance, but the owner of it, Hobey Beecham, was nowhere in sight, and Packy couldn't figure why this should be.

Why, he mused, would a rider want to leave his horse ground-reined out in the empty open, so distant from everything! And where the devil was Beecham, anyhow?

Almost with the question, Packy had his

answer. Hobey Beecham showed at the door of one of the cabins. There was an animal furtiveness in the way he peered so carefully out at the roundabout world. With a dirty bandanna he dabbed and mopped at his face.

Abruptly he lunged into the open and headed for the grullo. He moved bent over and hunched, as if he would keep as close to the earth as possible, fearful of being seen. The last few yards he covered at a run, startling his horse so that it backed and swung away from him.

When he finally got a hand on the dragging reins he hauled the animal savagely down and went into the saddle. He lifted the grullo to a grunting run, racing out the lower end of the meadow, sweeping past within twenty yards of Packy Devine without seeing him.

From his shelter behind the alders, however, Packy caught a good enough look at Beecham to wonder at the seeping blood and crimson welts which marked the fellow's heavy face and he pondered over this until the mutter of the grullo's straining run faded out to the south. After which he skirted the fringe of alders and sent the filly up meadow at a walk. He cut over to the cabin Beecham had emerged from and pulled to a halt. He listened for a little time then lifted a call.

"Hello — the cabin!"

There was no answer. There was no sound at all.

Out of nowhere a gray and ominous foreboding came to settle over Packy Devine. He dropped slowly from his saddle and stepped into the cabin. There he froze, staring, his face twisting and working. At first it was a sickness which rose in him. Then this was pushed aside by the sweep of human pity and a gust of cold, wrenching fury. From Packy Devine, an ever gruff, yet kindly little man, a cry blurted forth.

"Ah, the poor young thing — the poor, helpless young thing!"

7

All activity at Long Seven headquarters was pointed at the impending winter season. Case Ivy and Neal Burke, home from their weekend in town, were now back in the pin-oak ridges with the big Merivale ranch wagon, cutting and hauling wood for winter's fires. In the corrals, Hugh Carmack and Sam Hazle were sorting out the cavvy, deciding which horses would be kept up for the winter, which turned out on bigger range.

Perched on the top rail of the corral, Kelly Logan watched Carmack and Sam at their work. She was in her usual ranch attire of bib overalls, a boy's cotton shirt, and small half boots. Her hair was drawn back and tied so with a bit of ribbon. This etched her features sharply, and the glow of youthful health made them soft and pretty.

"Going to be her mother all over again," Carmack murmured in an aside to Sam Hazle. "Same hair, same eyes, same trick of wrinkling her nose a little when she's thinking about something."

It was Kelly who first sighted the approach of Packy Devine and called attention. Carmack and Sam crossed to the corral fence and leaned against it, watching Packy come on.

"He's running the filly harder than usual," Carmack observed. "Isn't like him."

Sam nodded. "Off hand, I'd say he was carrying some kind of word."

Packy saw them there at the corral fence and reined quickly up. It was as Carmack had remarked. The filly was blowing and its shining hide was dark and wet with sweat and there was a faint show of foam around the edges of the saddle blanket. These symptoms and a close glance at Packy's face told Carmack that Sam Hazle's conjecture was correct. Also, Sam could have added that the word Packy was carrying wasn't good.

"Riding a little further than usual today, eh Packy?" Carmack greeted. "You don't generally show here. Anything wrong?"

"Yes," said Packy, curtly somber. He glanced at Kelly. "It is not for the listenin' of a child."

Carmack stared an intent moment, then nodded.

"Run along, Kelly."

The youngster did not argue the point. She had grown up on this ranch where men accepted Hugh Carmack's quiet authority without question, and it had never entered her young mind to do otherwise. At times she had used childhood's privilege of teasing a bit for this or that, but also, with childhood's intuitive shrewdness, she could recognize the mood in Carmack when such delay was allowable. Other times, with that same shrewd perception, she knew when to obey wordlessly. Such a time was now. She dropped down from the fence and trotted off to other interests.

Carmack narrowed his glance on Packy Devine.

"Well?"

Packy told it exactly as it was. All that he had seen, all that he had found in the cabin after Hobey Beecham left. His voice ran out into huskiness as he finished, repeating words he had spoken earlier.

"— the poor, helpless young thing — !"

Listening, Hugh Carmack's first expression was one of incredulity, after which came a flood of black, wicked anger.

"You're sure she — the little squaw is dead?" he demanded harshly.

"Ay," affirmed Packy. "She is dead."

Sam Hazle began pounding a clenched fist on the corral rail.

"Beecham — Hobey Beecham! The dirty, low-down — !"

"You'll be riding back with me, Hugh?" Packy broke in.

"Of course. Both of us."

They caught and saddled and with Packy headed for the rancheria strip at a stiff pace, each man dark and hag-ridden by his own thoughts. In Hugh Carmack the fires of anger burned ever deeper, ever hotter, for though he was a steady man he was never a placid one.

The rancheria meadow was quiet and empty. Packy led them to the one certain cabin. They dismounted and went in. Immediately Sam Hazle began to swear in a soft, tight, droning way. When Carmack spoke, his words were equally toneless.

"It's the same one, Sam, who brought us the beef ribs at the Midnight Butte brush camp, yesterday morning. She was so shy — and in her own way — pretty — !"

The story of it all was plain enough. Signs of desperate struggle. Torn clothing. The pack Sadie Colo had been making up, now broken open, its meager contents scattered. Carmack took the blanket that had held the pack and spread it carefully over the crumpled figure. He tramped outside and built a cigarette, his face stony.

Sam swung a violent and vengeful arm. "Let's go get Beecham! Let's go — get — him!" The words ended on a rising note that left them little short of being a savage cry.

Carmack lit his cigarette, inhaled deeply several times before answering.

"Know how you feel, Sam," he said woodenly. "But the responsibility in this isn't just for the three of us. It belongs to the whole valley."

"You're not going to let Beecham get away with it, are you?" charged Sam. "You're going to do something — ?"

"Something? Of course. I'm going to hang Hobey Beecham!"

He took another deep drag on his cigarette, dropped the butt and ground it under his heel. He slid the Winchester rifle from its boot under his stirrup leather and handed it to Packy Devine, who had no gun of his own along.

"You're staying here, Packy. Nobody goes near that cabin until Sam and I get back. Nobody!"

Packy nodded. "That's the way it will be."

Leaving the rancheria strip, Carmack and Sam rode directly east, crossing Warrior Creek on to Cap McChesney's land.

Alone, Packy Devine stood for a time, considering some spot where he might be concealed, but from where he could maintain full view of the meadow and the cabins. He presently decided on a covert on the timber which fringed the meadow on the west. He tied the filly well back in the trees, loosened the cinch and spent a little time rubbing down sweaty flanks and shoulders with handfuls of pine needles and other dry forest floor duff.

He moved back to the timber edge within a few yards of where Sadie Colo had crouched while keening the meadow and the silent cabins before making her last short dash through the sunshine into a shadow from which she never returned.

Packy looked over the rifle Carmack had handed him. He put it to his shoulder and squinted down the sights. He cracked the action, saw there was no cartridge in the chamber and swung the lever fully to rectify this condition. He lowered the hammer carefully and laid the weapon ready to his reach.

In the main, Packy was a completely peaceful man. The gruffness of manner he affected at times was more a coverup of true kindliness than anything else. Though he would argue and bargain tenaciously to get the best of a horsetrade, he would cheerfully reach into his pocket at any time to feed a decent man down on his luck.

Basically he was a happy man and a cheerful one, seldom knowing anger. Yet this day he was charged with something greater than mere anger. It was outrage, cold, unforgiving, vengeful. He did not know how long Hugh Carmack and Sam Hazle would be gone, but however long the wait, he would hold his post here, guarding the cabin yonder and all that it held.

He had no idea who or what Carmack would return with. He knew only what Carmack had said he proposed to do. Hang Hobey Beecham! It was a grim objective which found full favor with Packy Devine.

■ ■ ■ ■

At Slash 88 headquarters, Trace Furlong was in foul mood. Possessed of a dark, introspective pride, he had brooded ever since the affair at the Pomo cabins. The fact that he had found the odds wrong and had let a streak of basic cunning steer him away from open showdown with Hugh Carmack, in no way alleviated the grinding truth that he had backed down. The knowledge was as salt on an open wound.

In this mood he was prone to exaggerate words or attitudes, to read in them more than was really there, and was quick to resent any slightest suggestion of his authority being flouted. And his feeling was that it had been by Hobey Beecham's attitude when ordered up to the rancheria strip to keep watch.

For Beecham, while not openly defiant, had been surly and reluctant, had grumbled and growled, and Furlong was anything but certain that his order would be fully carried out. It was not at all unlikely that Beecham, being thc sort he was, might have circled back to town after a load of whiskey and was now sleeping it off somewhere.

The mere supposition that this could be

so, further fed the smoldering fires in Furlong. Restless and driven by his thoughts, and with morning running along toward midday, he finally headed out for the rancheria strip himself.

He came into the meadow from the south and hauled up for a look around. All was quiet and there was no sign of Beecham or his horse. Which was all right, Furlong decided, feeling a little better about the matter. For Beecham had been warned to keep out of sight. Likeliest place to find him, if he was anywhere about, was in the timber yonder and Furlong reined over that way. He was some fifty yards from the trees when the order hit him.

"You can stop right there!"

Furlong set his horse up, lifting and forward leaning in his stirrups. His black eyes ripped sharply along the timber fringe.

"Who's talkin'?"

"I am — Packy Devine!"

Furlong eased slowly back against the cantle. Here was a thing to startle him and hold him mute for several long moments. Packy Devine, yonder in the timber and talking tough! In Trace Furlong's previous knowledge of him, Packy Devine was just a somewhat humble, mild little man who owned and ran a livery barn and corral and who would rather horse-trade than eat. Certainly there had never been anything very warlike about him. Furlong started on again.

The report of Packy's rifle was a sharp blare of sound, rocketing its flat echoes across the meadow. A yard in front of Furlong's horse a gout of meadow sod bounced and spattered and the horse reared back, wheeling and snorting. Furlong let out a startled cry.

"Easy — you fool — easy! What's the matter with you? What the hell's the idea?"

"The idea," retorted Packy from his covert, "is that you do as you're told. Stop where you are!"

To emphasize these words sounded the metallic ring of rifle mechanism as Packy levered another cartridge into the chamber.

Furlong fought his horse to reasonable quietness.

"All right — I'm stopped. But why this gun business? You here — with a gun — and hostile. I say — what's the idea?" Furlong's tone was tight with anger.

"My business," stated Packy, brief and blunt. "I'm in no mood for talk. Move out!"

Furlong searched the timber fringe with fuming eyes. This was adding gall to the wormwood. It was bad enough to be pushed around yesterday by Carmack and Hazle and McGah. Now to have a man like Packy Devine hold a gun on him — !

"You can't be hearin' very good, Furlong," Packy reminded. "I said — move out!"

Under the circumstances there was nothing else to do but obey. For a rifle bullet could be lethal, no matter who pulled the trigger that turned it loose. Even Packy Devine — !

"I'll move on," Furlong snarled. "But I don't savvy this. And when I do, maybe you'll wish — !"

Again the rifle report splintered the stillness and again a gout of sod leaped under the nose of Furlong's horse.

Furlong cursed bitterly as he fought down the nervous animal and made half a move toward his gun, a move he prudently and quickly corrected. For he had nothing to shoot at, while posing a wide open target himself.

"All right!" he yelled — "all right! I'm leaving. But answer me this. Is Hobey Beecham around?"

"Not here."

"Where is he?"

"Don't know. In hell — I hope. Now clear out!"

Trace Furlong spun his horse and spurred

back the way he had come. A wild anger was in him and he was of half a mind to swing wide and come up in back of Packy Devine, with a chance to throw a gun on him and teach him a lesson. Yet the very fact that it was Packy who lay hidden in the timber lent puzzlement and uncertainty to this whole thing which outweighed the anger and sent Furlong homeward at a reaching lope.

At Slash 88, with the lingering flavor of his midday meal still on his tongue and a fresh cigar burning between his teeth, Kirby Overton stood in the doorway of the ranch office and watched Trace Furlong ride in. The evident hurry of his riding boss and the manner in which Furlong set up at the corrals, left his saddle and crossed to the ranchhouse, put a frown of conjecture on Overton's face.

"Something," he greeted, "is eating at you. What is it?"

Furlong told him, growling. "Beecham wasn't anywhere around," he ended. "But that damned old fool of a Packy Devine was, and proud as hell with a Winchester."

"Packy Devine?" Overton exclaimed, definitely startled.

"That's it — Packy Devine."

"But you told Beecham to lay out there

and keep an eye on things?"

"I told him," Furlong nodded. "First thing this morning. I made it plain, too, for he didn't like the idea."

"And you're sure he was nowhere around?"

"Not unless he was dead. To warn me off, Devine laid a couple of slugs in front of me. If Beecham had been anywhere close the shots would have roused him."

Overton chewed at his cigar, his face hardening.

"I can't figure it," he said with a slow tautness. "I might guess that Beecham, being the stubborn, surly devil he is, could have got to feeling sorry for himself and cut for town after some whiskey comfort. But Packy Devine, lying out there with a rifle — that whips me. You say he threw some shots?"

"That's right. Ordered me the hell out and when I didn't take off right away, slapped a couple of slugs under my horse's nose."

Overton turned back into the office and Furlong followed, dropping into a chair and spinning up a cigarette. For a little time Overton stood, staring into space. Then he shook his head and sought his own chair.

"I can't figure it," he said again. "You got any ideas?"

"Nothing that adds up to sense," Furlong grunted.

"If it was anybody else," Overton mused, half softly. "But Packy Devine — out there with a rifle, warning people off — ! It leaves me nowhere."

"You think Carmack's been lining up backing anywhere he could find it?" suggested Furlong. "We know he aims to try and bring the Pomos back on the strip. Could be he's sold Devine on the idea."

"Yes, it could be," admitted Overton. "For I've always realized that past Carmack we'd meet up with considerable resistance of opinion from some people. But there is a lot of difference in holding an opinion and being willing to back it up in a showdown fight. I might see such as Marty McGah doing it. But Packy Devine — !" Overton wagged his head in disbelief.

"Tangles me as much as it does you," Furlong said. "What do we do about it?"

Overton lay back in his chair, sorting out ideas in a cloud of cigar smoke.

"If it was one of Carmack's crew I could figure it; it would make sense. Almost anybody but Packy Devine, it might make some sense. But him out there with a gun, even if he is siding Carmack — I tell you it leaves me whipped."

"Well, he's there," Furlong stated impatiently. "And with a gun. Do we just sit here chewin' our nails, or do we do something about it?"

"Presently — presently!" An edge came into Overton's tone. "This takes some thinking on, for there is more to it than shows on the surface. Couldn't you get anything at all out of Devine? Wouldn't he talk?"

"Damn little beyond telling me to drift. I did manage to ask him if Beecham was around, and he said no. I asked him if he knew where Beecham was. He said no again, but hoped he was in hell. That's the all of it."

Leaning, Furlong dragged a match across the sole of his boot and relit his cigarette.

"Sounds a little queer, what he said about Beecham," Overton reflected. "Not knowing where he was but hoping he was in hell. What reason would Devine have to hold anything against Beecham outside of maybe just not liking him?"

"Wouldn't know," Furlong shrugged. Then, with sly inference he added, "If you hated a man bad enough and he happened to be dead, you might say you hoped he was in hell."

Overton came erect in his chair, staring

narrowly at his riding boss. He jerked a curt nod.

"Now that is so. That is just so! And if such should be the case, then the gloves are off."

He got to his feet, crossed to the gun rack on the office wall and lifted down the shoulder holstered weapon hanging there.

"Put my saddle on a horse," he said. "We're riding, you and me."

Furlong also caught up a fresh horse for himself and they headed swiftly out. Overton had donned a light coat that covered up the shoulder holster harness, but could not fully conceal the slight suggestion of bulk beneath the left arm. Not that it was in his mind to hide the gun. It was simply a matter of personal preference to carry a gun this way when he felt the need of having one along.

There was a certain neat preciseness about this man to go with his florid, full-fed appearance. He wore his tall, white Stetson settled squarely on his head and he sat his saddle just as squarely. There was nothing casual or careless or easy about him, in dress, action or words. But always there was the impression that every move and item of his day was calculated and decided upon ahead of time. And behind this atmosphere of precise certainty in all things lay the suggestion of a power and purpose as thoroughly planned as it was effective.

Few men in the valley liked Kirby Overton for himself, but those who possessed little sentiment and were starkly practical, respected him for what he had accomplished despite his flair for ostentation in the way of possessions.

Their destination fixed, Overton and Furlong drove north along the creek trail, moving from one long-running meadow into another. Through these midday hours Slash 88 cattle moved in on the creek to drink and several files of them swung aside to let the riders pass.

In spite of the major question pulling at his mind, Overton made note of the number and condition of the cattle and knew a solid satisfaction with the answer. Sight of a beef critter of his own always affected him that way. For each of them bearing his brand was another item of proof of where and what he stood for in the world. Each was one more proof of possession, and to Kirby Overton, possession was his private god. Possession — !

Trace Furlong reined sharply in, staring down past his mount's shoulder at the hoof-marked meadow trail.

"Somebody just ahead of us," he warned. "Three or four of them."

He let it hang that way, waiting Overton's reaction.

"It's a free country," Overton said. "Go on!"

When they broke finally into the rancheria meadow, Furlong hauled up again. Four horses were grouped in front of one of the cabins. And Packy Divine, rifle across his saddle, was just riding out of the timber on the west.

"Must be something damned interesting in that particular cabin," muttered Furlong.

"Beecham, maybe?" hazarded Overton.

"Maybe."

They reined ahead. Glimpsing them, Packy Devine lifted the filly to a run and swung in at the cabin. He left his saddle and dropped the Winchester over his arm.

"Far enough!" he warned. After which he called something that brought Hugh Carmack, Sam Hazle, Marty McGah and Cap McChesney into view. After a brief look, Carmack spoke to Packy Devine and the threatening rifle pointed elsewhere. Overton and Furlong moved up.

From the eminence of his saddle, Kirby Overton looked over the grim faced group at the cabin door. That Carmack and Sam

Hazle should stand openly hostile, he could understand. But that Marty McGah and Cap McChesney and Packy Devine — especially Cap and Packy — should openly reflect the same feeling, was something to puzzle over. He studied them warily as he spoke.

"I'm looking for a rider of mine. Hobey Beecham. He in there?" He nodded toward the cabin.

A strangled ejaculation broke from Sam Hazle, but it was Hugh Carmack who answered.

"No! But something he left behind, is. Something for you to see!"

Overton's wariness deepened. This thing held him hesitant and suspicious. Now Cap McChesney spoke up, and the arrow-straight, white-haired old soldier's voice was as harsh and cold as polar ice.

"You heard what Hugh said. Get down!"

"That's it," seconded Marty McGah, silky soft. "Get down and have a look for yourselves!"

Overton shrugged and dismounted. With Furlong at his elbow he entered the cabin. The blanket covering Sadie Colo's mortal remains had been lifted aside. Blinking, Trace Furlong grunted as though struck a blow, and Kirby Overton caught a quick breath and let it out in a long, slow sigh. Behind them, Hugh Carmack spoke.

"You said you were looking for Hobey Beecham. Well, we are, too. You sure you don't know where he is, Overton?"

The question brought Overton around, anger flaring in his reply.

"Would I be looking for him if I did? Why should you want him? You're saying he had something to do with this? Who gave you that idea?"

"I did," said Packy Devine from the doorway.

Overton moved that way, out into the sunlight again. He paused and squared himself.

"All right," he said curtly. "I want to know about it. And I want to see some proof that Hobey Beecham had any part in it." His pale eyes bored at Packy Devine. "Who gave you the word?"

"Nobody gave me the word," Packy retorted. "I just know what I saw, that's all. And I saw Hobey Beecham slink out of this cabin, sneaky as a sheep-killing dog. And then he fogged it away like the devil was after him."

"Which proves what?" Overton rapped. "Not a damn thing! Beecham had orders to hit this meadow and keep an eye on things.

He could have been looking through the cabins. What he stumbled on here would naturally shake him up, the same as it would anyone. And he headed out to give the word."

"One big angle wrong with that story," Carmack said flatly. "Beecham didn't give the word to anybody. Not in town, and unless you're lying, he didn't give it to you. And if he didn't take the word to you or to town, where would he take it?"

Overton hesitated, then shrugged.

"I don't know. But I'm telling you this. I'll need better answers than any you've given me before I'll believe he laid a finger on that squaw in there."

"Rape and murder," said Cap McChesney coldly. "Ugly words for ugly deeds, Overton. We want that fellow Beecham. Where is he?"

"I tell you I don't know. Furlong and me, we just came through from headquarters, and Beecham wasn't there when we left. But let me tell you this. Wherever he is, he's a Slash 88 rider and I stand by my men. So don't go making any wild charges unless you can prove them." Overton turned on Packy Devine again, lashing words at him. "You know so god damned much — maybe you know more than you've told anybody

— more than you want anybody to know!"

Packy bristled at the inference, but Carmack dropped a hand on the little man's shoulder, restraining him.

"Packy's word is good enough for me. And, knowing Beecham, he's just the sort."

Overton, hating Carmack, stared at him, then swung his glance at the others.

"Got it all fixed up, haven't you?" he charged. "Yeah — all decided upon among yourselves. The word of a damned snooping stable hand is good enough for you. Well, it's not for me! Hobey Beecham is my man, and he's innocent until proven guilty. I'll defend his rights as I would my own. Come on, Trace!"

Overton stepped into his saddle and reined away. Trace Furlong silently followed.

Marty McGah turned to Hugh Carmack.

"Even if we needed further proof, Overton just gave it. He admits Beecham was ordered to stick around here and keep an eye on things. And if Beecham didn't do that, why didn't he?"

Carmack considered a moment. "The question supplies its own answer, all right. Sam, we have to get word to the Pomo camp, and you're elected. They'll want to take care of Sadie Colo in their own way. Make certain Bronco Charlie understands that justice will be done. He has our word for that."

"Yes," agreed Cap McChesney grimly. "Our word!"

8

When Hobey Beecham spurred away from the rancheria cabins, nothing slightly resembling regret or remorse rode with him. For these were emotions which the shambling brute in him denied utterly. Fear, however, was something else again, and fear sat on his shoulder.

Why this should be, he could not understand. So far as he knew, no one had seen him ride in or ride out. Why then, the weight of this fear? No answer came, and as he struck well down creek he reined west on to Slash 88 back range, seeking solitude while he reasoned this thing out. He hauled up in a sheltered timber pocket.

Clear thinking did not come easily, for at best his was a cloddish, ponderous mentality. An added handicap was the heavy load of whiskey he'd taken on while riding up from town. The bottle rolled up in the denim jumper behind his saddle cantle was barely half full, now.

In his time, Hobey Beecham had killed a

man or two. Also, he had mistreated women before. But never had he killed one — until now! This ugly fact pounded at his brain and stirred a panic in him. He began to sweat. For while you might kill a man and claim you did it to keep him from killing you and have such claim accepted — to kill a woman — even a squaw — ! There was something to put a curse on a man. . . .

It must have been the whiskey that made him do it, he decided. The damn whiskey! Yet, even as he cursed it, he twisted in his saddle and reached for more of it. He got the bottle free, shook it and held it up to measure the contents, then took a long, deep drag, shuddering as the heavy jolt hit bottom. It lay hot in his belly, and for a brief moment seemed to burn away some of the mist which clogged his mind.

Abruptly he knew what he had to do. He had to get rid of the dread evidence of his act. For if there was no evidence, then there could be no proof of anything. Yes, that was it. He had to go back and carry away the evidence. Maybe sink it in some deep, dark pool of the creek . . . or take it far back into the lava roughs somewhere and leave it where it would never be found.

But not just yet. He'd wait until he steadied down a little more. To aid in this process he took another heavy pull at the bottle.

He had a real capacity for liquor, but also he had his limits, and presently, when he took a third big drag, the whiskey, combined with what he had taken on earlier, peaked up and hit him. He swayed in his saddle, and, suddenly sleepy, began to blink, bleary and stupid. Yonder, at the base of a big fir tree a clear shaft of sunlight pierced through, spreading an area of inviting warmth.

He left his saddle, dropping the reins. Bottle in hand he crossed to the patch of sunshine, weaving, step unsteady. He settled down against the base of the fir and closed his eyes against the direct strike of the sun. He lifted the bottle and took another drink.

Right here, he decided foggily, he would stay and rest a while. Then he'd go get rid of — her —. Through the fumes that were drowning his brain he glimpsed a face, a young, brown face — twisted in terror and revulsion — the stricken eyes staring —.

He sucked on the bottle again and the fumes thickened.

He slouched lower and lower and began mumbling incoherencies. The bottle toppled over, most of the remaining liquor trickling out. He rescued the balance, cursing thickly. He drained the bottle and threw it aside.

He hiccoughed heavily several times and slumped over on his side. He began to snore.

From the rancheria strip, Kirby Overton returned directly to Slash 88 headquarters. There he had a look for himself in the bunkhouse, on the possibility that Beecham had returned to the ranch while he and Furlong were absent. The bunkhouse was empty. Overton questioned the cook and sent Furlong to check all the other ranch out-buildings. Nowhere was any sign of Hobey Beecham turned up. Now Overton paced the ranch office.

"You think he did it?"

Trace Furlong shrugged. "Be like him."

"The damned blundering animal! And he could also have spooked clear out of the country."

Furlong shrugged again. "Might be good riddance."

"No!" rapped Overton. "It's not that simple. He was part of Slash 88, and anything he did points at the whole outfit."

"Don't tell me you're sorry for the squaw?" Furlong's murmur was faintly sarcastic.

Overton threw up an angry arm. "Not for Beecham, either, even if the Lord should strike him dead. But I don't want any pack led by Carmack to get hold of him."

"What do you figure they might likely do with him?"

"A rope and a tree, probably."

"And that could still be good riddance," Furlong drawled.

"No!" differed Overton again. "Not that way. Not with Carmack over-seeing the job. I won't stand for him trying to police every move we make."

"Not just Carmack this time," Furlong said briefly. "Don't know when I've seen Cap McChesney looking any meaner. And that McGah — it's when he's extra soft voiced that he's the toughest. Might be a good idea to sit back and let them handle this in their own way."

Overton dropped into his chair.

"Hell with them! It's between Carmack and me, like always. As far back as I can remember he's been pushing in front of me, challenging my every act and move. I don't give a damn what Beecham did or didn't do — he's been a part of Slash 88, and if Carmack is after him, I'll stand by him, regardless."

"Then maybe we better try and locate him before they do." Furlong moved toward the door. "I'll hit town and see if I can pick up any word there."

"Do that," Overton approved. "And if you have no luck there, head out to our Sugar Loaf and Bitter Grass line camps for a look around. Could be Beecham sneaked out to one of them to lay low for a while."

Furlong paused in the doorway to build a cigarette. "Sounds like you figure friend Hobey guilty as hell."

"Don't you?" Overton shot back.

Furlong got his cigarette going and inhaled deeply. He showed the shadow of a cynical, twisted smile.

"Packy Devine is one of those rare fools who wouldn't know how to lie, even if he wanted to."

Saying which, he went away with dragging spurs, and presently hoof beats dwindled down the town trail.

Overton lit a cigar, the pressure of his irritation evident in the rapid way he puffed at the perfecto. While fully aware that there were probably others in the valley who owned little more real sympathy for the Pomos than he did himself, he also knew that certain crimes could stir a deadly anger in men, regardless. And it was becoming increasingly evident that Hobey Beecham had been guilty of such a crime. Which in no way bolstered the cause of Slash 88. Silently, Overton cursed Hobey Beecham.

As matters stood, however, with issues between Carmack and himself so strongly drawn, he would have to defend Beecham if the hulking rider should be come up with. For any other course would mean backing down in front of Carmack again, and that, Overton vowed savagely, he would never do!

He left his chair and renewed his restless pacing.

Shortly the rataplan of approaching hoofs brought him to the door. With his look he stiffened. Out there it was Hugh Carmack and Cap McChesney and Marty McGah who came riding.

They pulled up before the bunkhouse, looking warily around. A few words passed between them before they swung down. Carmack and Marty McGah went into the bunkhouse while Cap McChesney went over to the cookshack. All three reappeared shortly and crossed to the ranchhouse. Overton stepped out to meet them, pale eyes angry. While his glance touched Cap McChesney and Marty McGah briefly, it centered on Carmack.

"You got a hell of a nerve! Who gave you authority to prowl my premises?"

It was Cap McChesney who answered, his words clipped and bleak.

"You know why we're here. We're looking

for Beecham. He around?"

"No, he's not around."

"Do you know where he is?"

"No, I don't know where he is. But if he was here, you'd not touch him." He brought that remark back to Carmack, who shrugged and drily spoke.

"A point that could be argued over. However, though I don't know why we should, we'll take your word for it that he's not here."

"I don't have to give you my word on anything," flared Overton.

Now it was Marty McGah who spoke. "Seems a Slash 88 rider has turned out to be more animal than man. You'd best not be too proud of him, Overton, else folks might figure you approve of what he did."

"All I have to say to you fellows is what I said back at the rancheria cabins," Overton defied. "I don't know that Hobey Beecham did anything. And until it's proven definitely that he did, I'm standing by him. If he's guilty, and it can be proven so, then we'll call in the proper law authority from outside to handle matters."

"This doesn't concern outside authority," Carmack said. "This is a valley responsibility, and all the authority necessary is right here in the valley."

They headed back to their horses and Overton watched them ride away. He cursed Hobey Beecham again, this time aloud.

From Slash 88, Carmack and his two companions rode to town. Here, only from Russ Herrick in the Acme did they pick up any word of Hobey Beecham.

"He was in first thing this morning, right after I opened up," Herrick declared. "Had a couple of drinks, then bought a sealed fifth and headed out with it. That's all I know. Why all this interest in Beecham? Trace Furlong was around a little bit ago, asking about him, too. Pretty soon I'll be thinking Beecham must have held up a stage, or something."

"Nothing that decent, Russ," Carmack said briefly. He led the way out into the street again.

The day was far along. Late autumn haze lay like smoke along the rims and ranges, softening each distant butte and peak and hill shoulder into a lavender and powder blue fantasy, though carrying with it a suggestion of chill made real by the drift of air funneling along the street. Against this, Marty McGah hunched a shoulder while he twisted up a cigarette.

"Which leaves us where?" he murmured.

Carmack helped himself to Marty's

Durham and papers.

"What Herrick said ties in exactly with Packy Devine's story of Beecham being in town this morning after whiskey. And with Trace Furlong inquiring after him, it's plain that Slash 88 don't know where Beecham is, either. So there's nothing left for us to do but sit tight and wait, hoping he'll show up somewhere."

"Then you don't think he's cleared out of the valley?" Cap McChesney asked.

Carmack shook his head. "Doubt it. More likely, with all, or a big part of a fifth of whiskey under his belt, he's sleeping it off somewhere back in the timber. When he wakes up, first thing he'll want is more whiskey, and it wouldn't surprise me any if he came riding into town to get it. You know, Cap, we're seeing this thing through different eyes than Beecham is. Where the question of guilt is concerned, I mean. He knows what he did, but he doesn't know we know it. So, why should he spook?"

"But he was ordered out there to keep watch," Cap argued. "How is he going to square himself with Overton?"

"He doesn't know he has to, yct. Not that I think he would have to, for that matter."

Cap gave Carmack a narrow look. "Do you really see Kirby Overton as measuring up quite that short, Hugh?"

Carmack tipped a shoulder. "I know he raided the Pomos off the rancheria strip. During that raid one of the old Pomos was ridden down and died from the effects of it. Did Overton give a damn? Hardly! He went right ahead ordering the cabins torn down. After that would you expect him to know any concern over a stray little Pomo squaw? I'm just letting facts speak for themselves, Cap."

Cap slowly nodded. "They present a powerful argument." He glanced at the sun, almost down. "If there's nothing we can do but wait, I'll be heading home. But I have given my word that justice will be done and I mean to go through with whatever is necessary. Should you get a line on Beecham yet tonight, let me know immediately. Otherwise I'll see you tomorrow."

Erect, distinguished looking, Cap sought his horse.

Marty McGah hunched his shoulders again under the punishing breath of approaching evening.

"If we're going to wait it out here in town, I'm getting under cover."

Carmack sucked at his cigarette and spun the butt into the dust of the street.

"Leaving you for a time, Marty. I'll probably be back later."

"Where you going?"

"Same as Cap. Home. I'm not a foot-loose jigger like you. I got a family to look after. Got to see that Kelly's all right."

"And there you're luckier than you know," murmured Marty. "On your way, cowboy. Should Beecham show, I'll have him roped and hog-tied before he knows what hit him."

The sun was fully gone now and the world took on a raw, gray look. Marty rubbed his hands together and ducked back into the Acme. Carmack donned the coat tied behind his saddle, stepped astride and headed out. As he came even with Packy Devine's livery at the north end of the street, Packy rode in. Carmack hauled up beside him. Packy still carried Carmack's rifle. Now he returned it.

"I stayed on guard, Hugh, until Sam Hazle got back with some of the Pomos. Bronco Charley was one of them. They took the little squaw away with them. They didn't act no way hostile. Just — well, kinda lost and sad and hopeless looking. After they left, Sam headed for Long Seven and I came on to town. Damn! It's been a rough day — a mighty rough day. No sign or word of Beecham yet? I'd sure like to get a crack at that fellow."

"No sign yet, Packy. But we'll get him. Thanks for all you've done."

"Hell!" exclaimed Packy gruffly. "I don't need any thanks for acting the decent human being."

Some time after Hugh Carmack left town by way of the creek trail, Hobey Beecham, deep in his timber hideout, began to stir and emerge from the drunken sleep and whiskey stupor that had held him throughout the day. All trace of sunlight was gone and the timber was thick with bleak, cold shadow.

Consciousness did not come quickly; rather by slow punishing degrees. There was pain and thirst and nausea. Sledgehammers beat in Beecham's skull, hell-fire consumed his stomach and his mouth was foul. His eyes were like they were being forced from his head and when he finally got up on one elbow and stared blearily around, nothing would come into clear focus.

He shook his head and immediately flinched and groaned at the torment which whipped him. He spat, trying to clear the thickness from his mouth. Finally he sat up and braced his shoulders against the tree behind him.

Where was he? How did he get here? He was familiar enough with the after-effects of too much whiskey to know that he'd been drunk — very drunk. Now he had to figure out how and why and where?

Understanding, when it came, did so suddenly, and brought him lunging to his feet. His head seemed to explode and the world spun crazily and he caught at the tree for support. He stayed so for some time, waiting for things to steady down. But wild urgency was clawing at him. He had to get to the rancheria cabins — he had to get rid of that evidence — !

He'd slept too long, much too long. The whiskey — the damned whiskey — ! But right now he'd give anything for a big shot of it to straighten him out inside . . .

His horse — where was his horse?

Came the stamp of hoofs gone restless from inactivity and the bite of the cold gloom. Faithful to the tie of grounded reins the animal stood almost as Beecham had left it. He lurched over and with some difficulty gained a stirrup and then the saddle. By the time he made it he was shivering from physical misery as well as from weather chill. He rode to get clear of the timber.

Ordinarily, heading home from town, Hugh Carmack would have crossed Warrior Creek at Middle Ford and taken the east side trail to keep from riding over Slash 88 land. But this evening he kept to the west side trail, for there was a deep, depressed anger in him and a belligerency toward Slash 88 and all its works. So he would ride Slash 88 land and let any man try and stop him!

Lights were on at the Slash 88 headquarters, which he passed within a scant quarter mile. Dusk was short lived, with darkness close behind. Already stars like bits of splintered, cold fire were beginning to wink, and somewhere in the distance a great horned owl, early at a night of hunting, boomed its round and hollow note.

Weariness rode with Carmack, along with a sense of restlessness which would not let him relax. The picture of Sadie Colo's crumpled figure was burned on his brain, and knowledge of what had happened to her kept the anger seething and smoldering in him.

Vengeance? Of course! Why be a hypocrite about it? Sure he wanted vengeance. For Sadie Colo. . . .

Full starlight was a filtered glow across the earth when he rode into the rancheria meadow. Half way along he reined up, struck by the sense of desolation which blanketed the area. The still standing cabins were low crouched blots of blackness and there was a great emptiness all about. And a stillness.

But only for a moment. Over on his left there was sound and movement. Hoofs, dull-striking against the muffling earth, and then a shadow in the starlight which became horse and rider.

Prescience rippled through Carmack, bringing him up taut and leaning in his saddle, sharply peering.

That mounted figure yonder — that hulking figure!

Carmack's call rang harshly across the night.

"Beecham!"

Startled answer erupted in gusty exclamation, hoarse and unintelligible. Then the rider was charging away down meadow. Carmack set the spurs and drove in pursuit, racing in at a swift narrowing angle. From the fleeing figure a spurt of gun flame lanced, then another, the reports ripping wide the world's silence. As the angle of interception narrowed, Carmack drew his own gun.

Hobey Beecham threw a third wild shot, the flare of the weapon so close to Carmack's face it seemed he could almost feel the heat of it. Then, as his horse was about to crash shoulder to shoulder with Beecham's mount, he leaned and clubbed at Beecham with his gun. He felt the blow land glancingly.

Came the impact of collision. Knocked off stride, Carmack's horse floundered wildly, half up, half down. With the thought that the animal was going out from under him, Carmack threw himself clear. He landed hard, tripped and rolled. When he stumbled erect, two riderless horses were wheeling about with dragging reins, snorting their bewildered fright and edginess.

Over there a few yards distant, huddled against the earth's blackness, Hobey Beecham was groaning and mumbling in a dazed, incoherent way. Despite his upset, Carmack still had his gun. He closed in swiftly and again laid the weight of it across Beecham's head.

Hobey Beecham grunted and flattened out.

9

Before a well-used hearth where a fire whispered and threw out welcome warmth, Sherry Gailliard was curled up in a big rocking chair. On the table at her elbow a kerosene lamp with a brass bowl and hooded china shade gave off a yellow radiance. Night's deepening silence held the Gateway ranchhouse, for old Jeff Gailliard, victim of his physical infirmities, had already sought his bed.

The bit of sewing Sherry had been fussing with lay forgotten in her lap while her thoughts ranged far. Troubled thoughts, deeply troubled. For, shortly before sundown, Sam Hazle of Long Seven had ridden in to give brief word to Orde Dardin. Already plagued with knowledge of the tensions building between Long Seven and Slash 88, Sherry had wondered and been stirred to uneasiness by the subdued vehemence of Sam's manner, plus the abrupt way he rode in and out again. In consequence, she had called Orde Dardin up to the ranchhouse and asked what Sam Hazle's message had been.

Uncomfortable, embarrassed, Orde had told her. The sad and sordid facts surrounding the death of Sadie Colo.

"They're looking for Beecham," Orde ended. "Hugh Carmack, Cap McChesney and Marty McGah. Sam too, of course. They want us to keep watch, in case Beecham tries to skin out of the valley this way."

After the first sickening shock, Sherry's reaction had been one of anger, deep and outraged. Following this came realization that the all-over campaign of persecution against the Pomos by Slash 88, could very well have invited this ugliest of violences. And, when logically pursued, this same thought led to the inevitable conclusion that some of the fault at least, must be placed on Kirby Overton's shoulders.

That Overton would actually condone Hobey Beecham's crime, Sherry could not bring herself to believe; she had, she felt, known him far too long and too well. Yet there was no getting away from the fact that it was he who had ordered the initial raid on the rancheria strip and afterward sent men to destroy the cabins. No matter how you looked at it, these steps amounted to a letting down of the bars, thus encouraging further mis-treatment of the Pomos. Under the lash of her thoughts, Sherry stirred and sighed deeply.

A moment later she was swift from her chair and at a window, for the night's big silence had opened enough to let in the mutter of approaching hoofs. Across the interval she could see the yellow rectangle of a bunkhouse window, and now the bunkhouse door opened to show Orde Dardin standing against the light beyond.

That same light lanced out past him and across this narrow out-pour a mounted figure cut, then swung back again on a horse too restless from urgent running to come to an immediate full halt. Words passed between the rider and Orde Dardin. Sherry opened her window to listen. She caught the lingering fragment of a sentence.

"— in the Acme, tonight — !"

Again the mounted figure cut through the light beam and then the rush of hoofs was a diminishing echo. Orde Dardin turned back into the bunkhouse, but he did not close the door. By this, Sherry knew he was not going to stay inside.

She ran to the door, caught a wrap off a wall peg, then stepped into the night and hurried across the interval. The starlight was brittle with chill and the air stung her cheeks. Orde Dardin came out of the bunkhouse, pulling on a coat. Sherry challenged him.

"Orde — who was that rider?"

Startled, Dardin hesitated a moment before answering.

"Case Ivy of Long Seven."

"What did he want?"

"Seems Hugh Carmack caught up with Hobey Beecham and is holding him in town. They're going to try him tonight in the Acme. Hugh wants every outfit in the valley represented. I'm sitting in, if it's all right with you."

"Of — of course. What will they — Hugh — do with Beecham?"

Again Orde Dardin hesitated before gruffly replying.

"If he's proven certain guilty, probably hang him!"

Dardin went along to the corrals, where, in the cold, thin starlight, he caught and saddled and headed for town.

Sherry returned to the ranchhouse, stepped in and stood with her shoulders against the closed door while she stared across the room and saw none of it. Thoughts that had been merely plaguing before, now hammered at her with all the weight of a fast deepening crisis.

She was thoroughly a frontier girl, born under the canvas top of an emigrant wagon in a wilderness night camp. All her life she had lived in this far, lonely, lava-rimmed valley, and she knew the moods and makeup of its people. And when men rode urgently through the night to summon others to a meeting at which the life of another man was to be decided, then indeed was it become a valley full of threat and tension.

Abruptly she made up her mind. She hurried to her room and changed from house gingham to a wool blouse, divided skirt, boots and a fleece-lined coat. She tiptoed to the door of her father's room, listened to his snore and nodded her satisfaction. He was set for the night.

She crossed to the bunkhouse where Kenny Sharpe was playing solitaire. A solid, unimaginative young rider, to whom the tension of the night was of no particular moment, he was, never-the-less, a willing worker and thoroughly dependable.

"I'm going to town, Kenny," she told him. "Keep an eye on things. And you might put my saddle on that Oregon trail horse, the buckskin."

Short minutes later she was on her way. The buckskin fretted to run and she let it get rid of the first eager edge. After which it settled down to a mile-eating gait that was neither walk nor run, yet a little of both.

The night was vast and cold, and over all the land was a wildness which, in her childhood days, used to vaguely frighten Sherry, while holding and fascinating her at the same time. And she had never become unresponsive to it.

She tucked her chin deeper into the collar of her coat and from a pocket brought out a pair of worn buckskin gloves, which awakened a flicker of memory as she pulled them on.

Hugh Carmack had given them to her, three pair of them, a couple of years ago. He had bought a smoke tanned deer hide from one of the Pomos and had Henry Lindermann send it east to a glove making firm. Though not a grand gesture, it was, she mused, so like him, so indicative of his capacity for thoughtfulness and the unconscious ability to leave a touch of warmth here and there as he moved through the daily business of living.

For all this basic kindliness however, there was steel in the man, an unswerving adherence to the decent tenets of life and living. In such things he could be stern and severe and unyielding. He was not one to complicate his thinking, to dodge any issue by hiding behind soggy philosophizing which lacked direction and was made flabby by empty, mawkish excuses. With Hugh Carmack a thing was either right or it was wrong; it was black or it was white. Any mixture of the two produced a dingy gray which he despised.

It was this uncompromising attitude that had caused the numerous quarrels between the two of them. Even as far back as when they were kids, when Hugh Carmack thought she was in the wrong he told her so, flatly. And because she was fiercely proud and independent of thought herself, this never failed to infuriate her. And so their friendship over the years had been one of peaks or depressions; of, figuratively speaking, either laughter or tears.

Yet, in all fairness, Sherry knew the man was far less tolerant of his own shortcomings than he was with those of others. And even in her moments of deepest anger and resentment, she always recalled an observation she'd overheard Cap McChesney make one time while visiting with her father.

"Hugh Carmack," Cap had said, "is the kind of man some people do a lot of swearing at while he's alive, then build monuments to after he's gone. . . ."

At Middle Ford she crossed Warrior Creek, and here the night was layered thickly with the stream's wet breath. Across, and as she straightened out on the west side trail, she glimpsed a pin point of light in the Slash 88 bunkhouse, but none in the ranchhouse. Which meant, in all probability, that Kirby Overton was in town and would be present at the affair in the Acme. Which added fact posed an increasing possibility of further violence . . .

Sherry lifted the buckskin to a faster pace.

An under-current of tension as emphatic

as a shout met her when she entered town. It seemed that more than the usual number of lights gleamed along the street, as though here was something that was alive and of many eyes, poised and waiting.

Saddle mounts crowded the hitch rails, particularly in front of the Acme and Henry Lindermann's store. A shadowy group of men stood on the porch of the store, and as Sherry passed, their voices carried the hard growl of some kind of argument.

Sherry rode directly to the Mountain House, dismounted and tied. She climbed the steps, pausing at the top for another look at the street. As she did so a pair of riders whipped into town from the south and ran their horses quickly along to the already well filled rail at the Acme.

Sherry turned into the hotel and it was Maude Lawrence who came quickly to greet her.

"Sherry! For goodness sakes, child, what are you doing in town at this time of night? Something wrong out at the ranch? Your father — ?"

Sherry shook a quick head. "No, nothing like that. It's this other thing. Maude — you've heard?"

"About Hobey Beecham? Yes, I've heard. The town's been fairly seething, ever since

Hugh Carmack brought Beecham in."

"And if they prove him guilty, what they may do to him?"

"Hang him, you mean? They should!" Maude Lawrence declared. She softened her vehemence with an encircling arm and led Sherry into the hotel parlor. "Sit you down and relax," she went on. "For no matter how such as you and I might feel about this affair, there's nothing we can do about it. The matter will be decided yonder in the Acme, and that will be that!"

Sherry shrugged out of her coat and laid it aside.

"Yes," she agreed slowly, "that will be that. And, either way, it will not end there."

"Meaning, of course, the bad blood between Hugh Carmack and Kirby Overton," Maude Lawrence deduced shrewdly. "No, it will not end there, for Tip Marvin has been prowling and listening, and the word is out that Kirby Overton has vowed to see Hobey Beecham freed. It can't be he approves of what Beecham did?"

"How could he?" said Sherry quickly. "No, he couldn't approve. But it would be like him to defend Beecham, just to be opposing Hugh Carmack. You know, Maude, for a long time I believed the antagonism between Hugh and Kirby Overton was nothing worse than a dislike which would never lead to any extremes. Now I realize it is so much more than that. It's an enmity so implacable it frightens me. There's something dark and inevitable about it."

Maude Lawrence nodded. "Knowing men and the way the fires can work in them, I've long been sure of that."

"If there was only something I could do!" Sherry cried softly, striking her hands together in the familiar gesture of upset. "But I've tried talking to them both, and the moment I mention the subject they seem to move way off to some remote peak where I can't reach them." Half angrily she ended — "What is worse than a pig-headed man?"

"A pair of them. Yet," qualified Maude Lawrence, "I would not hold it against any man if he is pig-headed in the right."

Sherry considered a moment. "You're partial to Hugh, aren't you?"

"Yes, I am," admitted the older woman frankly. "And while I realize Kirby Overton has long been a friend of yours, too, I have to admit I have never cared for the man. There is a cold, inner self-concern about him which I can't abide. As for what's between Hugh Carmack and Kirby Overton, neither you or I or anyone else can do anything about it. As my father used to say about such things — they are fated, they are in the book. And no mere mortal can change what is already written. So, my dear, you and I are going into the kitchen and talk of more pleasant things over a cup of coffee. Come along!"

In the Acme men stood all along the bar and against the walls. At the room's inner end, Cap McChesney sat behind a poker table. He had taken off his hat and laid it on the table before him and under the down-pouring cone of light from a hanging lamp his hair shone whitely. His face was grave, his glance bleak.

At Cap's left, Hugh Carmack sat, while on the right, Hobey Beecham sagged in a chair. Behind Beecham, within an alert arm's length, Marty McGah impassively regarded the room and gauged its mood.

With Trace Furlong at his shoulder, Kirby Overton stood in the forefront of those at the bar. His feet were spread, his hat centered levelly on his head and a cigar was at a hard, combative jut in one corner of his mouth. Now he spoke past the cigar at Cap McChesney, his remarks challenging.

"Before this thing starts I want it known that I'm against it in all its parts. There's nothing fair or sound about it. It's a farce, cooked up by Carmack and you to make it appear legal."

Cap fixed him with a stern eye.

"It will be legal enough, Overton. There will be no frills and we will not be long about it. But our findings will be just and true. If Beecham is innocent, he will go free. If he isn't, responsible men will decide his punishment."

"What responsible men?" demanded Overton, sneering.

"There are plenty of them present," Cap returned. "I consider myself one of them. And if you have nothing better than a sneer to offer by way of argument, I suggest you keep your mouth shut!" Saying which, Cap turned his attention to the room. "We will now get on with the matter that has brought us here, gentlemen. The charge against Hobey Beecham is this!"

He gave it to them in curt, clear terms, without any unnecessary embellishment or softening of wording. Just the savage, brutal facts in the cause and manner of Sadie Colo's death. Most of those present had already had some word of the crime, but to hear it detailed in Cap's stern, precise way sent a sighing and a shifting and a stirring through the room.

When he had finished, Cap turned to Hugh Carmack and nodded. Carmack looked down the room.

"Packy Devine — step up and tell us what you saw!"

Packy stepped up and told them, stoutly and directly. "I saw Hobey Beecham come out of that cabin," Packy finished. "He was sneaking like a killer coyote and he headed out of the meadow at a run. The way he acted made me wonder. So I rode up to the cabin and looked inside. Cap just told you what I saw. So I headed for Long Seven to give Hugh Carmack the word."

"Which," charged Kirby Overton directly, "could have been a neat cover-up for yourself, Devine."

Packy came around on him, fast. "Meaning what, Overton?"

Overton shrugged, and let his remark hang.

Packy's cheeks tightened. "Should I lie, Overton — it will never be for the sake of my own hide. I'm different that way than you!"

Back in the crowd, Orde Dardin coughed significantly, and an angry glint showed in Overton's pale eyes.

"All right, Packy," soothed Carmack. "Now we'll listen to Beecham's side of it.

Speak up, Beecham!"

"He's lyin', of course," Beecham mumbled. "I didn't go nowhere near the rancheria strip until after dark, when I run into you."

"Why didn't you go there earlier — when you'd been ordered to?"

"Ordered?" cut in Kirby Overton sarcastically. "Was he?"

"He must have been," returned Carmack swiftly. "Else why did you and Furlong show there, looking for him. You said you were looking for him. Remember?"

Again Orde Dardin coughed significantly and the angry glint in Overton's eyes deepened.

Carmack went at Beecham again.

"If you didn't go to the rancheria strip, where did you go, Beecham? We know you came to town after a bottle. Russ Herrick will swear to that. And you didn't head back to Slash 88, else Overton and Furlong wouldn't have come looking for you. Where did you go?"

Hobey Beecham shifted uneasily and blurted his heavy reply.

"I took on more whiskey than I realized, so I drifted back in the timber to sleep it off."

"Why head for the timber?" probed Carmack. "Why not sleep it off right in the rancheria meadows?"

Beecham had no answer for this, so Carmack tried another approach.

"When you headed into the timber — what time would you say this was?"

Again Beecham stirred uneasily. "I dunno. How would I know? I wasn't paying no attention to time."

"Was it before or after you were in the rancheria meadows?"

"It was after — no, no — I mean — !" Beecham surged half out of his chair. "God damn you, Carmack — you can't trick me into saying I was somewhere that I wasn't. You — you — !"

Marty McGah dropped a hand on Beecham's shoulder and forced him back into his chair.

"Easy," drawled Marty. "Easy! Else I'll have to part your hair with a gun barrel!"

Beecham blustered wildly. "But that fellow Carmack — he can't make me say — !"

"He didn't make you say anything," Marty cut in. "He just kept asking you questions until you got tangled up in your lies and admitted the truth for a change."

Now Carmack went at Beecham relentlessly.

"So you were at the rancheria meadows

early in the day, after all, just as Packy Devine says you were. And it was after you were there that you hid out in the timber. Why that, Beecham — why that? Did you drain the bottle, trying to blot out memory of the thing you'd done? And when you came sneaking back to the meadows after dark, back to the scene of your crime — why did you run for it when I challenged you? Why did I have to ride you down and club you with a gun before you'd stop? Why all these things if you had nothing to hide, nothing to be afraid of?"

Sweat beaded Hobey Beecham's forehead, trickled down his cheeks. He mumbled thick reply.

"Lies — all lies! You're making it up. You can't prove a thing — !"

"We'll see about that!" Carmack rapped. "Quit staring at the floor. Get your head up, so everybody can have a good look at you. Tell me — the marks on your face — those deep scratches — how did you get them, Beecham? Or shall I say it? That Sadie Colo branded you with her finger nails when she tried to fight you off!"

Instead of looking up, Beecham lowered his head further. With an expression of vast distaste, Marty McGah grabbed a handful of Beecham's shaggy, greasy hair and hauled his head back, so that clear to the eyes of all were the scars Sadie Colo had inflicted, standing out in livid pattern against Beecham's sagging, sweat slimed cheeks.

Again a sighing ran through the room, and now it carried an undertone as menacing as a growl. At the sound, Hobey Beecham cringed.

Hugh Carmack got to his feet.

"I see no need of digging further into this matter. To me the facts are self-evident."

In the mind of Kirby Overton there had from the first existed little doubt of Hobey Beecham's guilt. Neither did he know sentiment either way where Beecham's future was concerned, or over Sadie Colo's brutal death. However, a gesture in Beecham's defense meant opposition to Carmack, so Overton put a question at Cap McChesney.

"Can somebody else beside Carmack offer a word or two?"

Cap regarded him grimly. "Certainly. Go ahead."

Overton swung to face the room.

"I still question our right to decide on a man's guilt and punishment under these rough and ready conditions. If Hobey Beecham is guilty as charged, let him be found so by an outside, legitimate court of law, and punished as that law provides. That is his legal right. I want every man here to ask himself if he'd be willing to be judged by such a deal as this. Ask yourselves that and then give me your answer!"

Nellis Coyne spoke up, and harshly. He was a big, raw-boned man.

"I'll give you my answer, Overton. This way suits me fine. An innocent man would have nothing to fear. But Beecham isn't innocent — he's guilty as hell! You know it and I know it. It stands out all over him. We don't need any outside court to tell us that."

"So you say," retorted Overton. "But there's the question of right."

Nellis Coyne made a hard, dismissing gesture. "That's empty talk. When have people like us ever needed any better right than this? It's our valley, and its affairs and responsibilities are ours, too. Some of us have women folk in our homes — I've two in mine. And any time the women folk of this valley, white or Indian, can't move or ride around as they please, when and where they please in complete safety, then I say it is high time we did something about it. And me, I stand ready to do that something, now!"

"Ay!" put in old Jim Garland, his ruddy cheeks showing no sign of his usual good nature. "Ay — that is so. Nellis is speaking for me."

"And here," nodded Cal Vining, normally the quietest of men. "My daughter Libby has the right to grow up in a valley that keeps its women folks safe."

There was little question of how sentiment stood. Hobey Beecham recognized this as thoroughly as did anyone else. He turned to Cap McChesney.

"Give me a chance!" He blurted desperately. "I'll ride out. I'll leave the country. I'll never come back. Just give me a chance — !"

From his place along the wall Sam Hazle jeered openly. "What chance did that poor little squaw, Sadie Colo, have? Beecham, your kind are all alike. You're big bold buckos until you're backed into a corner. Then you start yelling for the chance you never gave anyone else."

"That will do, Sam!" stated Cap McChesney sternly. "There will be no taunting of the prisoner." His glance covered the room. "This is a gathering of responsible men. You have heard — and seen the evidence. If any of you hold the slightest real doubt of the prisoner's guilt, I want that man to speak up." Now Cap's glance settled on Kirby Overton. "Well?"

Overton shrugged. "I've had my say. On

your heads be it!"

He turned and walked out into the night. Trace Furlong followed him. With their departure, Hobey Beecham saw his last hope fade. He yelled after Overton, cursing him.

"You told us to push the Pomos around — to rough them up. Damn you — you told us that!"

Cap McChesney stood, arrow straight, snowy haired, a stern, fine figure of a man, fully cognizant of what was soon to happen, and sobered by it.

"Very well, gentlemen. Give me your findings. Guilty or not guilty?"

The answer was a concerted rumble.

"Guilty!"

"And the punishment?"

There was the slightest pause. Then old Jim Garland spoke, simply and directly.

"Murder — and worse — was done by this man. There can be but one punishment. We all know what that punishment is."

Again came the concerted rumble, now of assent.

Cap McChesney looked at the prisoner. "Is there anything you wish to say?"

Knowing now that there was no hope, Hobey Beecham became fatalistic and surly.

"You can go to hell!" he mumbled. "All of you!"

Cap McChesney surveyed the room again. "As a group you judged this man, finding him guilty and proscribing his punishment. As a group you must witness this punishment. So long as it must be done, let us get it over with."

Not more than ten minutes later a long lantern dispensed feeble glow in Packy Devine's stable. That glow showed Hobey Beecham sitting on his horse. His hands were tied behind him and the rope noosed about his neck stretched tautly up into the overhead darkness. Round about, at the far fringes of the lantern's light men were more of shadow than of substance. Cap McChesney's voice came, grave and stern.

"Once more, Beecham. Have you anything to say?"

Beecham turned his head and spat.

Hugh Carmack stepped into the full glow of the lantern and swung a quirt.

The horse under Hobey Beecham surged forward, plunging down the stable runway.

In the overhead darkness a rafter creaked in protest against a sudden, swinging burden.

10

Most of them gathered again in the Acme, a quiet, grave-faced group. In particular was Hugh Carmack brooding and withdrawn. A grim and bitter business had just been concluded and now the settled, driving anger that had sustained him was burned out, and he slouched in a chair, feeling spent and empty.

Cap McChesney, carrying more years than the others, hovered over a glass of brandy at the bar, gaunt and tired and looking his years. Marty McGah, the philosophical, whimsical realist, seemed the least concerned. He put a glass holding a heavy jolt of whiskey on the poker table at Carmack's elbow.

"Now there is a bit of Russ Herrick's private stock. Wrap yourself around it, my friend, and it will wash the taste of today from your tongue. A man is bound to face up to some ugly things in his lifetime, and then, if he is to go on living with himself, he must carry through with the right as he sees it. There is only one question you must ask yourself. Was justice served? It was! So, drink up. As the wise man said — tomorrow is another day."

In a quiet threesome, Jim Garland, Nellis

Coyne and Cal Vining were having one for the road before hauling out on their long ride south to the Lost Prairie range. Never wordy men, they knew no need for such now. They had helped take care of a mean chore that needed doing. The world moved on and, as Marty McGah had just remarked to Hugh Carmack, tomorrow was another day. They put away their drinks and left.

Sam Hazle and Orde Dardin were together at the front end of the bar and now it was Tip Marvin who came in and spoke to Orde Dardin.

"Your boss is in town. Over at the hotel."

Orde was startled. "My boss?"

"Sherry. She wants to see you."

"What about?"

Tip Marvin shrugged. "Didn't say."

Orde shook a rueful head. "That girl! Might have known she'd come into town after I told her the word Case Ivy brought."

"Why didn't you do a little lyin' — the white kind?" Sam Hazle asked.

"Not me!" Orde declared quickly. "Not with Sherry Gailliard. When that girl looks you square in the eye, you feel like a bug on the end of a pin. You just don't tell her no lies, white or any other kind."

Orde put his drink away and hurried out.

Sherry and Maude Lawrence were waiting by the hotel desk. Sherry had donned her coat again, had one glove drawn on and was slapping the other restlessly across her gloved palm. Her face was grave, her eyes shadowed.

"So — it's over with?"

"Yes," Orde told her. "Over with."

"There was — no mistake?"

"You mean about Beecham's guilt? No, there was no mistake."

"And — they hung him?"

"In Packy Devine's stable."

"Was Kirby Overton there?"

"He was at the Acme. He tried to argue in Beecham's favor against Hugh Carmack and Cap McChesney. He didn't have a chance. When he realized he didn't, him and Trace Furlong pulled out, with Beecham cussing him and yelling that it was all his fault for starting the rough treatment of the Pomos in the first place."

"There could be more than a smidgin of truth in that," observed Maude Lawrence pointedly.

"I suppose," suggested Sherry soberly, "Hugh Carmack took the lead in things?"

Orde tipped a shoulder. "Somebody had to."

Silent a moment, Sherry nodded. "It would be like him. He'd never back away from what he felt was his duty, no matter what the cost."

"Which," stated Maude Lawrence with considerable force, "is one of the reasons I'm fond of him. Give me the man, every time, who is not afraid to stand up and be counted!"

Sherry pulled on her other glove, buttoned her coat and turned up the collar of it to warm and frame her cheeks.

"We'll go home now, Orde."

In the deep dark of the alley north of Henry Lindermann's store, Kirby Overton and Trace Furlong stood. From there they saw Sherry Gailliard and Orde Dardin ride by under the cold stars. A little later they watched Hugh Carmack leave town, along with Cap McChesney, Marty McGah, Sam Hazle and Case Ivy.

For a time after this group passed, Overton stood motionless, feet spread, head and shoulders swung forward in a pose charged with an unconscious arrogance. Trace Furlong, however, began to shift about, then made thin toned remark.

"Ever figure how one good bullet in the right place could solve a lot of things?"

"I have," Overton admitted slowly. "Plenty of times, in fact. Yes, I've often played with the picture of a set of gun sights lined up on that fellow, Carmack. It could come to such. Just how good a shot are you, Trace?"

"That could depend on how much money was in my pocket before I pulled the trigger."

"Suppose there was a thousand in your pocket — how good could you shoot?"

Trace Furlong drew in a quick, hissing breath.

"For a thousand — I couldn't miss!"

"Fine!" murmured Overton. "I'll remember that, just in case. But other things first. Tomorrow we start pushing cattle on to the rancheria strip, which should force friend Carmack's hand. He can't try and stop us without starting a fight. If he does, it could be that during the argument he'll fall off his horse and break his neck. Or — stop that slug you just spoke of!"

Furlong twisted up a cigarette, lit it and stared across the street at the shadow-black front of Packy Devine's stable.

"I wonder how Hobey Beecham felt when they put the rope around his neck?"

"Does it matter?" rapped Overton curtly. "Anyhow, it's something you'll never know. Let's move along."

They sought their horses and left town.

When they rode in at Slash 88, Trace Furlong took care of the horses, then headed straight for the dark bunkhouse and bed. In the ranch office, Kirby Overton sat alone for some time. The glow of the lamp at his elbow suggested a warmth purely illusory. For a past midnight chill filled the ranch-house and he slouched low in his chair, sifting his thoughts through cigar smoke.

Mainly did he go back over the attitudes and factors that had been present in the Acme. These had been far from comforting. In his attempt to stir up some sort of sentiment or defense for Hobey Beecham — not necessarily for Beecham's sake — but to test his own strength against Hugh Carmack in the lists of public opinion, he had found himself rather pointedly and disturbingly alone. Particularly in the feeling he had encountered in those he had felt would react differently, the men from the Lost Prairie range — Nellis Coyne, Jim Garland and Cal Vining.

He had known he'd find such opposition in Cap McChesney and Marty McGah, for these two were Hugh Carmack's best friends. But to encounter it so flatly and definitely in the Lost Prairie contingent had been considerable of a jolt.

Considering the nature of the crime, he knew now he had made a mistake in trying to defend Beecham. It would have been much better strategy to have declared against Beecham, to have voted him guilty and approved of the time and place and manner of punishment, even though it would have meant standing in agreement with Carmack.

Yes, he had made a mistake in not correctly weighing how Beecham's crime would be viewed by Nellis Coyne and Cal Vining and Jim Garland — men with women folk of their own. But how was he to know they wouldn't consider any Pomo as he did himself — as a being so far down the human scale as to be of no consequence?

He got to his feet and took a bottle and glass from the corner cupboard. He poured himself a stiff drink which warmed him and drove out much of the sluggishness of defeat he was beginning to feel. Also, it fed and stirred to renewed glow the coal of his ancient hate against Hugh Carmack.

This was a thing that had dominated his entire life. If such were possible, it had been at the same time a corrosive, yet constructive thing. Though it had colored his thinking with a lot of dark hours, it had also served as a driving force to lift him to his present position of power and possession. For, long years ago it was the hate that cemented the resolve to make himself a bigger man in the valley than Hugh Carmack.

In one way he had succeeded. Neither Hugh Carmack or any one else in the valley controlled more range than he, nor owned more cattle than bore the bold Slash 88 brand. And this house he sat in — where was there another in the valley to match it? Or a headquarters better laid out and better maintained?

Yet — !

A surge of dark inner feeling twisted Overton's face, coarsened it and made it ugly. Reason as he might, try by whiskey or any other means to drown it out, still there persisted far down in his being the realization that concrete possessions were not the full answer, nor of the consequence they might seem.

There was something else of far greater importance, which Hugh Carmack owned. It was a thing which could not be measured in terms of dollars and cents, of acres of range or head of cattle. It was an intangible, yet beyond all measurable price. When he possessed it a man rode high, very high in the saddle, and he threw a shadow that was long and wide. It was a strength which attracted other men. And women, too. It was a strong degree of character!

Basically lacking in it himself, it was the

nagging awareness of this fact that had contributed strongly to the antagonism and hate Overton had nurtured and kept alive down through the years. He would not admit it, even to himself, but it was fact, nevertheless.

He poured himself another drink, which fed the fires anew and turned his thoughts into another channel, in which he found no comfort. Sherry Gailliard had been in town this night, to of course hear of everything and know of everything. Thus, once again she had in effect witnessed another defeat on his part at the hands of Hugh Carmack. Further acid on an already open wound!

Had Kirby Overton been called up to define his true feelings toward Sherry Gailliard, he might have had some difficulty in making them lucid, so thick was the armor of his own self-concern. He had, of course, found a great deal of pleasure in her company, for she was a vital, spirited girl, good to look at, and while thoroughly feminine, still a true daughter of a vigorous frontier; one who could run her father's house, boss a ranch, and if necessary, perform most of its chores.

Being seen with her fed his ego and pleased his overweening sense of possession. Also, she would make a most fitting mistress of this big Slash 88 ranchhouse. In fact, the possibility of this had been at the back of Overton's mind when he first decided to build the place.

However, the last time he had faced Sherry he knew that in arguing defense of his treatment of the Pomo Indians and in trying to conceal his real intent toward the rancheria strip, he had lost ground in her eyes. Furthermore, his attitude toward Hugh Carmack had been challenged, and in the verbal exchange over this he had met Sherry's frank displeasure. Even more galling was her unconscious defense of Hugh Carmack.

Struck finally with the chill of this late hour and dogged by the taunting drift of his thoughts, Overton went to bed, taking the bottle with him.

In still another ranchhouse a single light burned late, as at Long Seven headquarters Hugh Carmack tried to shed the oppressive memories of the past sixteen hours. For though he knew with full certainty that justice had been served in the Acme and later in the runway of Packy Devine's livery stable, the raw ugliness of the entire affair from beginning to end, harassed a man with a persistent shadow.

He recalled the shocked pity he had

known for Sadie Colo, followed by a deep, remorseless anger toward her assailant. That anger had lasted through the capture, trial and execution of Hobey Beecham. But now it was gone, leaving in its place a chilled emptiness.

Carmack stirred up a fire in the ranch-house kitchen stove and put on a pot of coffee. While waiting for this to brew he went into Kelly Logan's room. By the faint glow of a low-turned lamp he had his look at the youngster. She was snuggled deep in the blankets, her hair a dark cloud on the pillow. One small cheek showed, flushed with sleep. Self-consciously and a little awkward in his gentleness, he leaned and brushed his lips against that warm cheek. After which, as he tip-toed from the room, he felt better about the day past.

He had built himself a cigarette and poured a cup of coffee when the back door opened and Sam Hazle stepped in from the outer night. The old rider threw a shrewd, quick glance and jerked a little nod of satisfaction when he saw that the hard set of Carmack's jaw and the lines of harsh feeling which had bracketed his mouth had now begun to soften and relax.

"Caught a whiff of that java cookin' and decided I could go for a cup of it," remarked

Sam gruffly.

"Sure," Carmack said. "Help yourself."

Sam poured himself a cup, cradled it in both hands and backed up against the stove's heat. Neither of them spoke again for some little time. Then Sam cleared his throat bruskly.

"Overton ran his nose into a post in the Acme, didn't he? Couldn't find no support nowhere. Ought to slow him up some."

Carmack considered soberly, then shook his head, "I doubt it. He can't afford to stop now."

"He can't afford to try and fight the whole valley, either," argued Sam. "And Nellis Coyne and Jim Garland and Cal Vining — they threw his talk right back in his face."

"Because he was trying to defend something that was indefensible. With another issue, like what stands between him and me, they'd likely be strictly neutral."

"How the hell could they be, between you and such as Kirby Overton?" Sam growled.

Carmack smiled faintly.

"You could be a mite prejudiced. Jim Garland and Cal Vining and Nellis Coyne are hard-headed, practical, realistic men. Their primary concern is for their families ahead of everything else, which is as it should be. They took a common stand tonight because they were judging a man guilty of something unforgivable. So they were willing to share the responsibility of taking care of him. Beyond that, while they might, deep down, own an opinion one way or another, they're hardly likely to mix in with something that doesn't strictly concern them."

"How about the deal Overton's been throwing at all the Pomos?"

Carmack shrugged. "Same thing. I'm not saying they approve, understand. But everybody doesn't feel toward the Pomos the way we do, Sam. If we keep to the west side trail, then every time we go to town we cross rancheria land. They're our next door neighbors and we see them fairly often. But the Lost Prairie outfits, being way south like they are, can go six months at a time without laying eyes on Bronco Charley or any of his people. And there is nothing truer than the old saying — 'Out of sight, out of mind.' "

"But all those people came through with some old blankets for the Pomos. Shows they have some sympathy there."

"Of course they have. Still and all, sympathy has its limits."

"Sadie Colo was a Pomo," Sam persisted.

"And — a woman," Carmack pointed out.

"A lone and helpless one. Which makes the difference. No, Sam — whatever comes up strictly between Slash 88 and us, is a ride we'll make by ourselves."

Sam mused for a time, sipping his coffee. "I reckon," he agreed presently. "What's Overton's next move — drifting cattle?"

"That's it. Onto the rancheria strip. He's made his talk. If he doesn't have a try at making that talk good, then he admits he's whipped before he starts. The only way he can make it good is move in and occupy — take over our range. To do that, he has to come across the rancheria strip first. So — !"

"And we argue?"

"Of course!"

Sam drained his cup. "Rough times ahead."

"Yes," Carmack admitted.

Sam spun up a cigarette and moved to the door, a pale thread of smoke trailing across his shoulder. He paused with one hand on the doorknob.

"This is shaping up like the old days. Yes, sir — just like the old days. Well, they do say human nature never changes, which is why history repeats itself."

Alone again, Hugh Carmack built a final cigarette before seeking his bed. Physically, he was completely weary. But though the inner tumult of feeling had largely quieted, there was still a restlessness in him. It took time for all the tensions to entirely drain away.

Soberly he calculated the reverberations that would be aroused by the lynching of Hobey Beecham. Word of it would certainly cross the mountains in time, but he doubted any particular reaction from that source of outside law. For the valley was remote and had always been allowed to run its own affairs in its own way.

More immediately, there was Sherry Gailliard to be considered. She would be thoroughly outraged at Hobey Beecham's crime. But whether she would approve of how the rest of the ugly matter was carried out, was something else again. If she didn't, he mused ruefully, she'd certainly not hesitate in telling him so with emphasis.

He stretched, yawning. He picked up the lamp and headed for his room. There was no point in worrying, one way or the other. What was done, was done. A man did what he had to, and then stood on the result and accepted what came of it.

11

He awoke to an acute sense of weather change. Daylight's first touch at his window was gray and furtive and there was the whine of wind about eaves and corners of the ranchhouse. He dressed quickly and headed for the kitchen, pausing at Kelly Logan's door when she called sleepily to him. He went in and looked down at her and met a warm, sweet, drowsy smile.

"Stay put, youngster," he told her. "Old Man Winter is snorting at the gate. You stay snugged in for a time. I'll stir up a fire in the kitchen for you to dress by. Benjy will hold breakfast for you."

He stoked the stove full and stood for a little time soaking up some of the gathering heat. After which he had a good wash, donned hat and coat and stepped out into the push of the wind. It came in from the south and carried a cold, wet smell. A rack of leaden clouds hazed the sky and over east, along the hump of the Barrier Hills, the haze lay particularly thick and dark.

In the cookshack Benjy Todd had the lamps burning against morning's gray gloom, and the place was savory with the breath of breakfast. Carmack took off his hat and coat and backed up to the far end of the stove.

"Snow on the ground within a week," Benjy prophesied.

"Yes," agreed Carmack. "Could be sooner."

"Tough on the Pomos if they got to face it in a brush camp."

"Maybe we can get them back in their cabins before it starts."

"Won't that have to be argued out with Slash 88 first?"

Carmack nodded. "Likely enough. If we have to, we will." He spoke quietly, but Benjy did not miss the tightening line of his jaw.

"Sam told me all about yesterday and last night," Benjy went on. "Proud of you, boy. A dirty job that had to be done and you didn't back away from it."

There was the stamp of boots at the cook-shack door and a man's coughing against the new day's raw chill. Sam Hazle came in and went over to the wash bench. He doused and sputtered, used the towel vigorously, then smoothed down the grizzled thatch of his hair with gnarled fingers.

"You aim to keep cow critters off a certain chunk of range, it could be a heap easier done if you stop 'em before they get on it instead of letting them light and then have to root 'em out again. What do you think?" he rumbled.

"You got a point there," Carmack agreed.

Case Ivy and Neal Burke came in and washed up. Right after, with a hop and a skip, Kelly Logan came through the door, her dark hair neatly braided, her fresh washed cheeks glowing. She stood beside Carmack and leaned against his arm.

"Thought I told you to sleep in," he scolded gently. "No need you getting out this early."

"I wanted to eat breakfast with you," she stated simply. "I don't like to eat alone."

The remark stayed with Carmack as they took places at the table. It was, he realized with some feeling of guilt, an angle he hadn't thought too much about. The increasing periods of time when this youngster would be left increasingly alone. For the demands of ranch work never lessened, keeping him and the crew out and busy in the saddle.

True, Benjy was always around headquarters, but the cookshack was his castle and he knew little activity beyond its limits. And an empty ranchhouse could be a vast and lonely place for a nine year old youngster, no matter how self-sufficient she might be in her own small way. He recalled what

Maude Lawrence had so recently said about Kelly's right and need of council and companionship of a woman, and could not dodge the truth of it.

Also, he considered what loomed immediately ahead. The specter of all-out conflict with Slash 88. This day, even, the issue could become one of gunsmoke. A shadow of anger stirred in him. Why must such things be? Why should Kirby Overton be as he was, and why should he, Hugh Carmack, own that fierce, driving inner need to always oppose Overton?

He shook the frustration of these thoughts from his mind and came back to the immediate concern for Kelly's welfare. He tipped his head beside her small one.

"How would you like to visit with Sherry Gailliard for a few days?"

There was a quick start of eagerness in shining eyes and parted lips.

"She said she wished I would when she was here the other day, Uncle Hugh."

"Fine! And it best be before a storm sets in. Soon as you finish breakfast you run along and roll your pack. I'll catch up Pepper and you and I will ride over to Gateway."

Kelly wasted little time finishing eating. Then she was out and gone. Benjy Todd banged a skillet on the stove.

"We no sooner get her back from visitin' in town, you send her packin' off somewheres else. Leaves the ranch empty as a washed out gulch."

"It's what's best for her that counts, Benjy," Carmack soothed. "We got something ahead of us that could turn bad. Some of it might even reach here to headquarters. Should that be so, I don't want Kelly here. At Gateway she'll be safe and happy. When things quiet down again we'll have her back."

Sam Hazle nodded his complete agreement, then asked:

"What's for today?"

"You called it when you came in. When I get back from Gateway we'll drift down to the rancheria strip and patrol a little."

"Case and Neal and me might as well head that way now," suggested Sam. "You can meet us there."

Carmack considered, then nodded. "All right. But don't get into any unnecessary trouble."

"Any trouble we get into will be necessary," Sam promised.

The morning was much too bleak and raw for Jeff Gailliard to take his usual place on the ranchhouse porch, so Sherry settled him in the living room before the hearth fire, knowing a pang at the renewed evidence of his increasing physical infirmity. And she could so easily remember when, as a little girl, how he had seemed such a giant, who would sweep her up effortlessly with one hand and balance her on his shoulder. How bitter must be his portion to have once known that kind of strength and vigor and now be tied to what amounted virtually to an invalid's chair. It was easy to understand why his mood should be so crusty and crochety these days.

The breath of winter was definitely blowing upon the world, and Sherry hated to see it come, for as she had told Hugh Carmack, it was the cruel season. It meant long weeks of being cooped up indoors, of loneliness and physical inactivity. She was thinking of this now as she looked out the window and saw Carmack, accompanied by a small, well muffled companion, come riding across the meadow from the creek ford. There was a sizable bundle tied behind Kelly Logan's small saddle which suggested something that quickened Sherry's mood to eagerness. She swung wide the door to greet them, Carmack carrying Kelly's bundle and Kelly beside him, smiling shyly.

"You asked for this," Carmack said. "You

told Kelly you wished she'd come visit you. Well?"

"Wonderful!" exclaimed Sherry. "A day, a week, a month — six months! Welcome and more welcome. Come in — come in!"

She hugged Kelly, helped her out of her coat and muffler and led her in to the crackling hearth and to the gaunt, bony-faced man seated before it.

"Father," she said, "here's Kelly Logan, come to visit with us."

Jeff Gailliard peered from beneath grizzled, shaggy brows, marking the glowing cheeks and the limpid directness and beauty of Kelly's little girl glance. A smile softened the grim line of his lips.

"Come near me, child," he said.

Kelly moved over to him and surrendered her hand to him. He patted it gently.

"I hope you stay with us a long, long time," he said.

Watching from the doorway of the room, Sherry turned back to Carmack, murmuring, a faint break in her voice.

"She won him with a single glance. Childhood and age. Always there seems to be an affinity, an understanding between the two. Hugh, it's good of you to bring her."

"Good of you to make her welcome," Carmack returned. "Saves me some worry."

Tone and words made her look at him sharply. "Saves you worry?" She went on, deducing shrewdly, "It's because here she'll be well away from any possible trouble?"

"Partly," he nodded. "While deserving other companionship than any offered her at Long Seven. We do the best we can, but she needs the feminine touch, too."

"That trouble," Sherry probed. "You feel it might strike that close to home?"

Carmack shrugged. "You never know about such things."

"And there is no way of getting you and Kirby Overton to agreeing on a lasting truce of some sort?"

His glance took on a hard directness. "What do you think?"

She looked away. "After — after yesterday, and after last night, I don't know what to think. Hugh, you've no regrets?"

"Only for Sadie Colo. She deserved something better from life."

She brought her eyes back to him, studying him for a sober moment. She nodded the acceptance of an inevitability.

"The stubborn steel is there and always will be. It's useless to argue against it."

Carmack grinned, thereby seeming to shed several years.

"You make me out a very tough fellow.

And you know I'm not."

Sherry tossed her head. "You will always go your way, regardless."

"As far back as I can remember," he said quickly, "I've hoped you'd be willing to go right along that way with me. I'm still hoping."

She colored warmly. "The way we fight? Life would be one long argument. Within a week we'd be scratching each others' eyes out."

"Better that with you than a lifetime of sweet peace with anybody else," he insisted.

She tried a light laugh, but it was far from steady.

"Hugh Carmack, you pick the darndest times and places to say the darndest things . . . !"

"Don't I though! Like the first time I said you were my girl, way back when you were still in pig-tails."

Before Sherry could think up fitting reply to this, Kelly came away from Jeff Gailliard and claimed her hand.

"The other day you said I could sleep in the room you did when you were a little girl. Can I see it, please?"

"Bless you — of course!" Sherry exclaimed. Over Kelly's head she made a face at Carmack. "Best say goodbye to your

Uncle Hugh. He's leaving."

"That's right," grumbled Carmack, "kick me out!" Then, glimpsing Kelly's look of concern, he added swiftly, "It's all right, honey. Sherry and me, we're just funning each other. And I have got work to attend to."

He leaned for Kelly's hug and kiss, then turned to leave. Sherry accompanied him to the door.

"Kelly," he said, "is more generous than you."

Again color built high in her cheeks, again she tossed her head. "That's because she doesn't know you like I do." But as she closed the door on him she added with quick gravity, "Be careful, Hugh."

Carmack re-crossed the creek at the Gateway Ford, then turned south along the west side trail. In the small interval of time he'd spent in the Gateway ranchhouse the wind had switched to the southeast and turned strongly boisterous. The gray canopy overhead had thickened and lowered. No longer was this cloud cover a flat sheet, instead it now boiled down from beyond the Barrier Hills in great surging billows, full of a wet and threatening breath. Carmack untied the slicker from behind his saddle cantle, opened it and shrugged his shoulders into it as he rode. Five minutes later the first gust of rain struck.

A wet, bitter day lay ahead, which fact Carmack accepted stoically. But it was no day for cheerful thought, however, for added to the immediate physical discomfort was a lingering residue of yesterday's grim shadow.

Gloomy forebodings were easily fomented. Like considering the crime and punishment of Hobey Beecham, which, while in itself a thing apart, emphasized how far the effects of an almost feudal hate between two other men might reach. Carried to a logical conclusion, had such a feeling not existed in the first place, then the Pomos would not have been driven from their rancheria, and there would have been no need of Sadie Colo's solitary return, and Hobey Beecham would not have been there to trap her.

Carmack swung restlessly in his saddle. You could, he thought bleakly, trace the impact of such enduring hate on and on into any number of consequences. It was like the dropping of a single lighted match which could start an inferno. And when such happened, who knew where, or how far the flames might reach?

He considered his own crew. Like Sam Hazle, getting on in years and deserving a chance to spend the balance of them peacefully. And Case Ivy and Neal Burke. Younger men, especially Neal, entitled to a good future without being called upon to face any hazards beyond the legitimate ones of their saddle trade. And while a fidelity to their outfit and a willingness to fight for it was all well and good, and a part of any good rider's philosophy, it was in no way fair to expect them to assume additional risks just to back him up in something that had started a long, long time ago between himself and Kirby Overton. No, not fair to ask them to share an animosity so intensely personal between Overton and himself and which rightfully, should be decided strictly between them — man to man!

Only it wasn't that simple! For a man's obligations did not necessarily begin and end entirely in himself. He, for instance, had Kelly Logan to consider. Her need of him in all ways was paramount. Yet, the way things were shaping up there was no certainty in his future, either. Nothing, it seemed, could be reasonably certain or planned on while Kirby Overton lived.

That was it! That was what all the coldly brutal facts boiled down to. While Kirby Overton lived, there could be no peace.

Unless, of course, Overton could be

persuaded away from his avowed intentions by more peaceful means. Perhaps, after the demonstration of feeling he had met with last night in the Acme, he might, as Sam Hazle had suggested, have been convinced he'd better go slow. However, in Carmack's opinion, this was a slim hope, more a matter of wishful thinking than anything else.

The rain swiftly became a settled downpour and cloud mists swept low along the creek meadows and through the timber flats, to hedge in a man with their clamminess and shrink the sweep of his vision. Head bent as he drove straight into the cold lash of the rain, Carmack now began to doubt any attempt would be made by Slash 88 to move cattle under these conditions. The sensible thing for him to do, he decided, was to locate Sam and Case and Neal and all head back to the dry comfort of the Long Seven bunkhouse.

He came into the rancheria meadow and saw the low bulk of the Pomo cabins huddled in the mists. Maybe Sam and the others had sought shelter in one of these. But along the whole length of the meadow he saw no sign of the men he was searching for, so he rode on further south, heading for the Slash 88 line. What with the drive of the rain and whip of the wind, it seemed he could see little and hear less. But abruptly his senses registered in both ways.

Bursting through the mists just yards ahead, came half a dozen head of white-faced cattle. They were running heavily, leaving behind the rumbling bellow of complaint. They passed Carmack close enough so that he could, despite the rain and mist, read a brand. No mistaking it. /88. Slash 88.

And the sound! The thin, high echo of a rider's yell, followed by the thump of several gunshots. These came in from Carmack's right and he swung his horse that way, using the spurs. Came another rattle of shots, so smothered and muted by the storm it was hard to judge their number or exact location.

He drove into a fringe of timber where branches lashed wetly at his low-crouched shoulders and bent head. Then he was through and into another open and there were cattle all about him, scattering like a covey of quail. Also, beyond the cattle were riders, two of them, and one of them saw Carmack and yelled warning.

There was no mistaking the owner of that high, hard, carrying yell. Trace Furlong!

Furlong held a gun and he threw down on Carmack. But his horse was whirling and jostling among the cattle and the shot flew wild. Carmack tried for his own weapon, clawing aside the wet, stiff skirt of his slicker. Before he could do any good, Furlong and his companion were gone, racing into the misted timber beyond.

Case Ivy came charging in from the west, rifle free and ready, yellow oil-skin slicker streaming wetness. His voice rang savagely as he hauled up beside Carmack.

"Where'd they go — Furlong and Riff Powers? They dropped Neal back yonder. Where'd they go?"

Carmack pointed, but stopped Case with a harsh word, when he would have gone on.

"No! Don't try it. They'd trap you in the timber and you wouldn't have a chance. Neal — he's dead?"

"I don't know. Sam's with him."

"Let's get back there. Lead out!"

"There were two, three others with Furlong and Powers, but they skinned out quick. Only Furlong and Powers showed fight. It was Furlong who knocked Neal down." Case's voice turned uneven with bitter anger. "By God — I want that fellow in my sights. Just one good shot — that's all I want. Just one good shot!"

Neal Burke was flat on his back on the soggy earth, his eyes shut, his young face pale and drawn from shock and beaded thickly with the driving rain. Sam Hazle was on one knee beside him.

Carmack was swiftly out of his saddle. "How bad?" he demanded.

"Bad enough," reported Sam. "In the right chest."

Neal Burke stirred, opened his eyes, managed a crooked smile.

"Useless," he murmured. "That's me — plumb useless. Had to stop a slug, first chop."

"You shut up!" Sam charged gruffly. "Save your strength for something better than talk. You got a slug in you that has to be dug out, and it's going to hurt like hell both before and after."

Sam drew Neal's slicker closed again and got to his feet. "Where do we take him? Home, maybe?"

Carmack shook his head. "Not with that kind of a wound. Too many things it can lead to. It's got to be town and Doc Blair as quick as we can get him there."

"Considerable ride," Sam said doubtfully. "Think he can make it?"

"With me holding him in the saddle, he can. Anyway, we got to try it. Give a hand, Case!"

Between the three of them they lifted Neal

Burke into Carmack's saddle, where he sagged, only partially conscious. While Sam and Case Ivy held him so, Carmack swung up behind the saddle. He looped an arm about Neal, hauled him close and held him braced that way.

"All right!" he rapped. "Now we go. Case, you line out ahead. Tell Maude Lawrence to have a room ready and get hold of Doc Blair. Give him some idea of what to expect and have him waiting there, ready to get to work. Sam, you bring Neal's horse along and stick with me, in case we bump into any of that Slash 88 crowd. And, Case — you keep clear of them, too. No hunting further trouble just now. Plenty of time for that — later."

Case Ivy drove away at a run, was soon lost in the storm. With Sam Hazle out ahead of him, leading Neal Burke's horse, Hugh Carmack turned his face into the rain and set his mount to a fast, swinging walk. In the circle of his arm, Neal Burke sagged loosely, a gravely stricken young rider. To hold him secure required a steady, lifting support. Without that support, Neal would have slithered from the saddle like an empty sack.

Anxiety clawed at Carmack. This was the very thing he had thought of, and feared, during his ride down from Gateway — that Neal or Case or Sam might pay the supreme penalty for something no way their concern or fault. Yet, here was Neal already victim, perhaps with his young life draining out of him. . . .

Carmack shook his head, bitterness building up in him, pulling his face into coldly dedicated lines, knowing now what he was going to do, knowing now what he must do.

It became a wicked ride. The wind surged more heavily and turned colder. Abruptly there was more than chill rain striking at Carmack's cheeks. Snow flakes began to wing down, spectral and ghostly, and the mist cloaking the world, thickened and grew paler.

Except for several bunches of cattle they saw nothing, met no one. The cattle, drifting before the storm, paid them no attention other than to part ranks grudgingly and let them through, then plod on, heads low, rumps to the driving white smother of the snow.

Long before town was anywhere near, Carmack's arm and shoulder went dead, with Neal Burke that loose and sagging weight, until Carmack began to wonder if he could last, himself. Worst of all, he now had no idea whether it was a live man or a dead one in the saddle before him. What with the cold and the physical drain, something almost like a stupor gripped him, and he had to pour out every ounce of strength and concentration he possessed to last out this thing.

And it was when he was at the utter edge of strength and will that he suddenly became aware of buildings bulking on either side of him, and here, either because the buildings broke its full force, or because his own sensibilities had become so numbed he couldn't tell the difference, it seemed the wind had lessened. He was pondering this with faculties gone slow and groping when he found Case Ivy down there afoot, holding his horse by the rein and swinging it back to a hitch rack already partially passed.

Case called to someone: "He's so beat out himself he don't know where he is."

Then it was Case and Doc Blair and a couple of others who were lifting Neal Burke down and carrying him away. And it was Sam Hazle offering a helping hand, helping him down, too, steadying him on feet that felt like lumps of unfeeling stone, then steering him across the street.

"Damn rough ride, that," Sam growled. "Rough as hell all around. I know what both of us need. This way!"

"Neal?" mumbled Carmack. "How about — Neal — ?"

"Being cared for best way possible. There's nothing more you or me could do — except get in the way. Come along!"

Sam shouldered open a swinging door and then they were in the Acme, met by a wave of warmth that rolled over them with a beneficence that was almost pain, it was so welcome. In a far corner of the long room a big cast iron stove creaked with heat, and on top of it a kettle simmered and sang.

Russ Herrick, staring for a startled moment, came quickly out from behind the bar.

"Something wrong? Hugh hurt?"

"No." Sam pushed Carmack into a chair, took one himself. "A mite tuckered, is all. He just done half carrying a man plumb from the rancheria strip. What he needs most is a little rest and some warming up. A good stiff, hot whiskey toddy would help like hell — him and me both. So mix a couple. We'll tell you what happened, later."

Herrick set to work swiftly and soon the toddy was in Carmack's stomach, the warmth of it spreading. It relaxed him, cleared his brain and quickened his blood. He began swinging his left arm back and forth, swearing softly at the pain of a million darting needles of renewed feeling piercing and reviving numbed flesh and nerves as the arm and shoulder came alive once more. He rubbed the chill from his cheeks and motioned Herrick for a refill.

"All right," he said presently. "How did it happen, Sam?"

Sam, becoming loose and relaxed in the sheer luxury of warmth, inside and out, sprawled in his chair.

"We just bumped into them, is all. We hit the strip and began patrolling it. For a time we didn't hear or see anything. Then, when we swung west, closer to the Slash 88 line, we were all of a sudden plumb in the middle of a jag of cattle, with maybe half a dozen riders pushing them. Surprise was sort of mutual, I guess. But Trace Furlong was there and he didn't waste no time in going tough. Whether he was surprised into it or acting under orders, I dunno. Anyway, he threw a gun, quick — and dropped Neal."

Sam took another long drag at his toddy and went on.

"The shot spooked the cattle, started them running in all directions. And damn an oil skin slicker! One may help keep out the rain, but it can sure muffle up a man when he wants to move fast. Anyway, by the time Case and me got unwound enough to do a little shooting, it was mainly by guess and by god, what with the rain and confusion, with cow critters and riders ducking this way and that into the mist. We didn't hit nothin' that I could see. Case, he lit out after a couple of those jiggers, while I got down for a look at Neal. Time I located where he was hit and found that he was still alive, you and Case showed. That's the picture."

"You're certain Furlong threw the first shot?"

"Hell — yes! No question. He didn't wait to ask no questions or to say I, you, or but. Acted more like he was a damn rustler, or something, caught redhanded. Just threw a gun and knocked Neal out of his saddle."

Russ Herrick, who had been listening closely, made brief comment.

"Sounds like him, all right. A mean one, Trace Furlong. Don't give a damn for anybody or anything. Just himself. How bad is Neal Burke hurt?"

"That's something we'll have to wait Doc Blair's word on," Carmack said.

The saloon owner fed a couple more chunks of wood into the stove from the stack along the wall.

"After yesterday and last night, now this," he said slowly. "Hate to see it start up, range trouble. Most generally it never accomplishes much beyond hurting a lot of people, most of them innocent. Why in hell would Overton want to put cattle on the rancheria strip — ain't he got enough range already?"

"When was enough ever enough for one like Overton?" returned Sam Hazle curtly. "Besides, have a look at what's on the other side of the strip. Us!"

Russ Herrick stared, his eyes slowly narrowing. "So that's it!" he murmured.

"That's it," nodded Sam.

Herrick mixed more toddy. "On the house," he said, handing over the glasses.

With fingers reasonably supple again, Carmack built a cigarette. Sam borrowed the makings and did likewise. Cloaked in a waiting somberness they smoked in silence.

The minutes ticked away, ran into half an hour. Sam got up, went to the door, pushed it partially open and stared out at the storm. He shook his head, came back and resumed his chair. A little later Packy Devine came in, shrugging a sprinkling of snow from his coated shoulders.

"I put your horses under cover, Hugh," he said. "They're tied in the runway of my stable. Heard about Neal. What's the word on him?"

"We're waiting for it," Carmack told him.

Another full half hour went by before Case Ivy came stamping in. As one, Carmack and Sam pushed erect, their question unspoken but demanding.

"Doc Blair got the slug," Case reported. "Says the chances are about even. Depends a lot on whether complications set in. Says it could be tomorrow before he can make a sound guess. If Neal does make it, Doc says, it's mainly because of the time saved by getting him straight to town."

"Doc needing any more help?" Sam asked.

"No. I offered, but Doc said there wasn't anything anybody could do that him and Maude Lawrence couldn't do better. Looks like just a matter of waiting."

"Then you and Sam better line out for headquarters," Carmack decided. "Benjy Todd is there alone, and somebody ought to be with him, just in case, now that this thing has busted wide open. I'll stay on here for a time and be along, later."

He gave Sam and Case enough time to be well on their way. Then he tramped down to the stable, got his horse and headed out. But his destination wasn't Long Seven. It was Slash 88.

12

Of the men of the valley, only Jeff Gailliard and Captain Rufus McChesney were veterans of the savage, bloody war between the states, so they were of a brotherhood apart and when together spoke a language meaningful to themselves alone. Because Jeff Gailliard, with his infirmities could not travel, Cap McChesney made it a point to ride in at Gateway every now and then to spend an hour or two with an old comrade in arms.

It was so this gray and stormy morning. Quite some time after Hugh Carmack splashed across the Gateway ford and disappeared down the west side trail, Cap McChesney came riding through the rain along the east side.

Sherry met him at the door. To her, this ramrod straight old cavalryman, with his careful speech and courtly manners, his stern face and snowy hair, would ever epitomize the romance and color of the old and valiant days.

"It is very kind and thoughtful of you to visit father on such a morning, Captain," she said, taking his dripping hat and faded old military cloak. "Go right along in by the fire."

Cap McChesney bowed slightly.

"My dear, it is ever a pleasure to step into your home. One reason I'm here is because of the kind of morning. For a real storm is building up and it may be some time before I can come again. Mrs. McChesney asked me to convey to you her respects and best wishes."

"And you must carry mine back with you," Sherry returned.

From the kitchen, Kelly Logan edged shyly into sight. Cap McChesney smiled at her.

"Another visitor present, I see."

"Hugh Carmack brought her to us this morning," Sherry explained. "She is to stay with father and me for a time and we are all very happy about it. She won father with a glance."

"Which I can easily understand," declared Cap. "Childhood has ever possessed a direct, unaffected charm peculiarly its own. Mrs. McChesney and I have often expressed our wish that we might have had such a youngster in our home. Hugh is lucky in his role as foster-father to her."

"Yes," Sherry agreed, then added soberly, "Before you leave, Captain — I want to speak to you about Hugh — and others."

Cap gave her a quick, narrowed glance.

"Very well."

He went into the living room and Sherry heard the deep growl of her father's welcome. She carried Cap's hat and cloak to the kitchen and hung them close to the stove to warm and dry. She brewed a fresh pot of coffee and had Kelly deliver a cup of it to each of the old soldiers.

Through the kitchen window she saw the rain turn to snow and she thought of Bronco Charley and his Pomo people in a brush camp over by Midnight Butte. She thought of why they were there and a deep sense of anger began to stir in her and she went at her household tasks a little fiercely.

Later on, Cap came into the kitchen. "What was it you wished to speak of, Sherry?"

She gave Kelly a little pat. "Go keep father company for a little time, honey."

Afterwards, Sherry faced Cap directly.

"It is this thing between Long Seven and Slash 88 — between Hugh Carmack and Kirby Overton. You were in town last night, Captain?"

"I was," Cap nodded. "I might remark also that justice was done."

"But it won't stop there?"

Cap considered, lips pursed, then answered slowly.

"I doubt it. A fact that worries me increasingly."

Sherry exclaimed. "You and others! It has me half crazy. The worst of it is, I feel partly responsible."

"You — responsible? Oh, I see." Cap noted the swift color warming Sherry's cheeks. "My dear, it is never a woman's fault if two men become enemies through a rivalry for her affections — not unless she deliberately plays them, one against the other. Which, of course, you would never do."

"I'm not too sure I haven't done exactly that," Sherry said carefully. "Not realizing it, and of course not meaning to. But doing it, just the same."

"How could that be?"

"Ever since we were children," Sherry explained, "Hugh Carmack has warned me — cautioned would be a better word — against Kirby Overton. Which, of course, has always infuriated me. I don't know how many times Hugh and I have quarreled over that particular point, with me resenting the inference that I was not capable of forming proper judgements by myself, nor choose my own friends as I pleased."

"Quite understandable on your part," Cap agreed drily. "Also on Hugh's."

"How do you mean, Captain?"

"Why, that Hugh is an excellent judge of character. I wonder if you're not ready to agree with me on that?"

Sherry stared out of the window at the white curtain of snow before meeting the keenness of Cap's glance.

"Perhaps I am," she admitted. "Which is why I wanted to speak to you like this. I've done my best, talking to both Hugh and Kirby Overton, trying to clear things up between them, and haven't gotten anywhere. When Hugh feels he is in the right, then nothing can sway him. And —."

"Isn't he right in this affair?" Cap cut in.

"Yes, he is," Sherry admitted again.

"Then should we expect him to change? Or want him to? On the other hand, I doubt we can do much with Kirby Overton."

"I was going to ask you to see Kirby, Captain. Surely he must respect your opinion."

"He didn't last night," said Cap crisply. "Not mine, or that of anyone else. He was arrogant and defiant. In the face of evidence beyond all argument, and against the judgement of virtually all present, he tried to stand in favor of that unspeakable lout, Hobey Beecham. Even so, it was my feeling that actually he did not care a finger snap for Beecham, but was out merely to obstruct, to be in opposition to Hugh Carmack, regardless."

Cap paused, his lips tightening slightly before he went on with a note of harshness.

"I would never deny any man the luxury of a good, stout hate, providing it be an honest, healthy one. But the other kind, the malignant sort, based mainly on corrosive envy, is something else again, and that is the way it is with Kirby Overton. He is not, and never could be, half the man Hugh Carmack is. Which fact he fully realizes and it is eating him up inside. It is like an incurable distemper. In my time I have seen several afflicted that way, and nothing short of death ever changed them."

Sherry flinched. "Then you feel it is no use talking to him?"

"I'm afraid not," Cap told her honestly. "Yet, because you ask it, I'll make a try. On my way home I'll stop in at Slash 88. And I'll have another cup of coffee before I leave."

At the Slash 88 a lamp in the office fought back some of the day's cold gloom. A corner stove spread welcome heat and backed up against this, Trace Furlong steamed as he made his report. From his chair at the desk,

Kirby Overton listened, peering through curling tobacco smoke with narrowed eyes.

"And you downed young Burke?" he probed as Furlong finished.

"Pretty sure it was him. Right about then the weather was mighty thick, what with the rain and mist."

"He wasn't alone?"

"No. At least two others with him. Afterwards, Riff Powers and me, we bumped into Carmack further along. For all we knew there could have been more somewhere around. In the mist it was hard to tell who was who and who wasn't. I tried a shot at Carmack, but my horse was spooking right then. So I didn't hit him."

"Didn't they shoot back?"

"Some, but with no luck. I'm telling you, things were real mixed up about then."

"But you did put some of our cattle on the rancheria strip?"

"Damn right! Maybe sixty, seventy head. With the storm on their tails they were traveling good. They'll drift back into the timber and in this kind of weather there'll be no easy digging them out. They should be there for the winter."

Overton took another long pull at his cigar and smiled thinly.

"Good enough! Every time we get any

break in the weather we'll put more in the same place. Come spring we'll own that strip, Trace. And after that — Long Seven!"

Stirred by the prospect, he got to his feet and took a turn up and down the room.

His thin, dark face sultry with thought, Trace Furlong sucked on a limp cigarette, and spoke slowly.

"Spring's considerable off. Just as much time for Long Seven to do things as us. Wish it had been Carmack I downed instead of Neal Burke."

"Well, I'll certainly go along with that," Overton said. "Maybe next time, better luck."

"There could be a lot of next times," declared Furlong. "Up to now, Long Seven and us, we been like a couple of dogs walking around stiff legged, plumb full of growl and snarl, but not quite wound up enough to take first bite. Well, now the trigger's been pulled and the first bite's been had."

Overton paused in his pacing, eyeing his foreman narrowly.

"For someone who just got away with that first bite, you seem a little gloomy."

Trace Furlong shrugged. "I'm taking a good, full look at what could lie ahead. I got no more use for Hugh Carmack than you have, but I'm not blinding myself any to the fact that he can be a mighty rough customer when he takes off the gloves. Hobey Beecham found that out, last night."

"Forget Hobey Beecham!" Overton said sharply. "He was a blundering fool."

"Fool or not, he was hung last night," retorted Furlong. "Which ain't easy to forget. And it was Carmack, more than anyone else, who hung him."

As he spoke, Furlong had crossed to the office window and glanced through it at the stormy world. He stiffened and stared. Out there a rider was moving in on the place, and though outlines were somewhat vague through the blur of falling snow, recognition struck.

"For God's sake! It's Carmack, riding in!"

Kirby Overton stepped up to peer through the steam misted window pane. "Yes — Carmack. Now, why — ?"

Furlong, quickly to the far side of the room, caught a rifle down from the wall rack. Overton warned him off.

"Easy! No need of that."

"Last night you talked a thousand dollars worth." Trace Furlong swung the lever of the gun, lifting a cartridge into the chamber. "I want that thousand." He started for the outer door.

Overton got there first, barring his way. "I

said — easy! Would you be a bigger fool than Beecham?"

"You want him down, don't you?" Furlong demanded. "Ain't that what you said — that you wanted him down?"

"Off somewhere deep in the timber, yes. But not in our front yard. Put the rifle back."

Reluctantly, Furlong obeyed, and Overton gave him no chance to argue further.

"Go out the back way. Keep out of sight until Carmack's in here. Then get over to the bunkhouse and bring Riff Powers here with you."

Furlong shrugged and made his way back through the ranchhouse.

Presently bootheels struck up muffled echoes along the porch and Carmack's knock sounded at the outer door. Overton's summons was curt.

"Yes?"

It had been his thought to carry this thing off from the eminence of his office chair, thereby emphasizing not only a complete enmity, but also a derisive contempt. However, when the door opened and he looked up at the man who stood there, he knew a quick thread of panic. It was as if he were being overwhelmed. Never had Hugh Carmack appeared so tall and broad. He seemed to fill the doorway. Overton came to his feet, to cut down some of the disparity in stature.

"Well!" he rapped, feigning surprise, "Mr. Carmack himself! The last person I ever expected to see in this house. I can't imagine what brought you here, and you understand of course, that you're anything but welcome."

Hugh Carmack shrugged. He whipped the clinging snow from his hat and shoulders, tramped over to the stove and spread his hands to the heat. He looked gaunt and his face reflected a brooding weariness. For the moment he seemed content to just stand by the stove in silence.

Kirby Overton watched him, puzzled. "You've got something on your mind, else you wouldn't be here. What is it? Say it — and get out!"

Carmack came around to face him.

"I came to see if there wasn't some middle ground where we could meet and head off any more trouble between us."

Real surprise widened Overton's eyes, followed by a wary, sardonic glint.

"Now there is a considerably different sound to what you've been spreading the past few days. I don't quite get the change of tune, Carmack. What are you reaching at, anyhow?"

Carmack dug tobacco and papers from a pocket and fashioned a careful cigarette before answering.

"Neal Burke, one of my boys, is lying in town with a bullet hole in him. Doc Blair says it is fifty-fifty. Neal got that slug out of a ruckus that you and I have brewed up, down over the years. Yeah, he got it on my account, and I don't want him or anybody else to take any more punishment for that reason."

"You stand quite some bigger of heart this morning than you were last night," charged Overton, openly sarcastic.

"Not so," Carmack differed. "For what he did, I'd have seen Hobey Beecham hung, had he been riding for me instead of you. He was no damn good, which you know as well as I do. As a man, he wasn't to be compared with Neal Burke."

"So you say," Overton retorted. "One thing is certain. Burke wasn't riding the rancheria strip just for the hell of it. He was there with others, to make a try at keeping me from working some cattle in there. A thing I've the legal right to do, the strip being government ground." Overton's banked feelings began to show, his voice lifting, his words coming faster. "You keep your men out of my way, they won't get hurt. Don't come crying to me because one of them did. You ordered Burke on to the strip, I didn't."

"Yes," murmured Carmack, half to himself, "I did order him in there. For which I'm sorry. I was wrong in doing it."

Overton stared, his short laugh carrying a note of incredulity.

"Can I be hearing right? The rough, tough Mister Carmack, beginning to crawl? Backing down at the first whiff of gunsmoke? And he was the one who was going to save the world for the noble red man. Carmack, I thought better of you than this — I really did. While I've always hated your guts, I did give you credit for having some. Yes, sir — I will be damned!"

"You will be — and you are," Carmack said, quietly and evenly. "You're jumping at conclusions — taking things for granted — doing some wishful thinking. Which is always dangerous business. I'm not crawling, Overton, and I'm sure as hell not backing down. Nor have I in any way changed my intention to see that Bronco Charley and his people return to the rancheria strip, while you get off and stay off. What I came here for was to notify you that the game was going to be played different, from now on. I'm not going to ask anyone else to handle any part of a chore that is so definitely my chore. I'm going to handle all of it myself. I'm going to see that this affair is settled right where it should be — just between you and me. Nobody else."

"Now you are getting proud," taunted Overton. "You'll run Slash 88 off the map all by yourself — is that it?"

"You're still not listening good," Carmack said. "I just told you it's all between you and me. You have the choice of getting back into line and staying there — or taking the consequences."

"Consequences! What consequences?"

"Showdown!" Carmack put the word flatly. "Between you and me. Nobody else. It's our feud. It's always been our feud. And if I have to kill you to settle it, once and for all — that is the way it will be."

Abruptly, Carmack's glance was lance-level and charged with a harsh, boring intensity. Overton met it for a moment and then his eyes slid away. His cigar had gone dead and soggy and he tossed it into the wood box. He got out a fresh one, lipped and lit it carefully, using the interval to get his thoughts reorganized and straightened out.

Very definitely had he jumped at conclusions, and misjudged Carmack's initial attitude and remarks. Which had been a mistake, and it meant that once again, in a battle of wits and words he had come off second best.

This gaunt, somber-eyed man in front of him was in deadly earnest. A thread of caution told Overton he'd best listen and be guided accordingly. However, crammed as he was with the long accumulation of grinding hate, plus the bitter gall of a perverted sense of pride, he pushed caution aside and a snarling bluster swelled in him.

"You got a hell of a nerve — throwing that kind of talk at me in my own home. And it doesn't scare me. For a showdown can work both ways!"

Now Overton cocked his head slightly, as though to listen. Some of the twisted tension drained out of him and a mocking smile creased his florid cheeks. "All right, Trace!" he called.

The inner door of the room swung, letting in Trace Furlong and Riff Powers. They drifted quickly apart, their attention strictly on Carmack. And Overton eyed him tauntingly.

"What was all this about a showdown? Still proud, Carmack?"

Carmack's expression did not change. His glance touched Furlong and Powers briefly, then came back to Overton.

"I've had my say," he observed bluntly. "I'll stand on it."

Buttoning his coat he moved to leave.

"Not so fast!" Overton rapped. "Watch him, Trace!"

Trace Furlong drew a gun. Carmack hauled up, watching him narrowly.

"Put that away, Furlong — before it gets you into real trouble."

Furlong waggled the weapon slightly. "You heard it. Not so fast!"

Carmack shrugged, looked at Overton. "You got anything that makes sense, get it said. Else I'll be going."

"Maybe you will," Overton said. "Maybe it's not that easy. Not for you to ride in here, throw your weight around, threaten me, then ride out again, big as hell. No, maybe it's not quite that simple!"

Carmack shrugged again. "Something you propose to do?"

"I'm thinking," Overton murmured. "Yeah, thinking. How any man has the right to defend his own home. And if somebody comes into mine, threatening to kill me, where would I be to blame if that somebody ended up dead. You see how it could be, Carmack?"

Carmack's cigarette was cold in his lips.

He crumpled the butt between his fingers, let the fragments drift away. Again his glance swung, touching each of these three, gauging their true intent. Riff Powers, being purely the instrument of Overton's order, presented the least problem. He might do as he was told, but he would not act of his own volition. He had no ax to grind aside from the fact that he rode for, and drew his wages from, Slash 88.

On the other hand, Trace Furlong was thoroughly unpredictable. Turned loose, either by order from Kirby Overton, or by the streak of innate savagery so plainly visible in him, Furlong could be all killer, cold-blooded and ruthless. However, it seemed hardly probable he'd go all the way at such time and place as this without direct order from Overton. So all would rest with Overton.

Thus Hugh Carmack's thoughts ran as he looked at these men in turn and measured them. From Riff Powers to Trace Furlong to Kirby Overton. Here his glance fixed with sudden intensity. For, with a sense of real shock, came the feeling he was looking at a man he no longer knew!

Enemy though this man Overton had been down through the years, it had always been Carmack's belief that he could read him pretty thoroughly, and thus know what to expect of him under a given situation. That Overton could be rapacious and ruthless, when he felt time and circumstance warranted, had long been proven. But also, he had ever displayed a calculating caution against definitely committing himself as an individual. While he might order some extreme act, he was careful not to mix in the act personally, or would he be, unless absolutely necessary, present at the doing of it.

No such caution was showing now. Plainly, the last extreme was in this man's mind. Carmack could read it in the hard, hating glint of Overton's eyes, and in the snarling pull of his lips. Kirby Overton did not intend that he leave this room alive!

One brief moment of an entirely natural fear touched Carmack and then fatalistic acceptance of the situation took over. And a quickening alertness, cold and bright, charged his nerve ends.

He backed up a stride, so that he might have all three of these men in better focus. He regretted having buttoned his coat, which would now slow him in a try for his gun. Yet he would have to make the try. Maybe if he moved fast to one side — and kept on moving. . . .

Seeming to read the thought, Trace Furlong crouched slightly. In Carmack, every tingling sense was suddenly raw with the need for action; for release from a tension that had, in short seconds, become almost unbearable.

At the outer door of the room a knock sounded, and it struck through the tension like a thunder clap.

Trace Furlong twisted, hissing like a startled snake. Riff Powers swung to face that way, too. And Carmack made the most of the opportunity. Two long, lunging strides put him close to Kirby Overton, and he was drawing his gun as he moved. He jammed the muzzle of the weapon hard against Overton's ribs. Breath broke from him, gusty with relief.

"Now," he charged harshly, "we'll see!"

Came a second knock at the door. Then it was pushed open and the tall, spare, snow-powdered figure of Captain Rufus McChesney stood there.

"Overton," said Cap bluntly, "your manners are rotten. Haven't you the common courtesy to invite a visitor in out of a storm?"

Stepping from the outside world into this room of strain, Cap needed a small interval of time to absorb the significance of what he saw before him. His voice rang again, sharp and demanding.

"What's going on here?"

"Nothing, now, Cap," Hugh Carmack said. "For a time friend Overton was playing with a real wild idea, but I think he's changed his mind. You too, haven't you, Furlong?"

Fully aware that Cap McChesney's unexpected presence had halted this thing in its tracks, Trace Furlong shrugged and put away his gun. But he met Carmack's mocking glance with a hard insolence which hinted of other days and opportunities to come.

In his time, Cap McChesney had been through too many tight corners not to recognize an atmosphere of threatened violence. He recognized it and its significance now.

"Hugh," he said, "you were foolish to come here!"

"Yes," agreed Carmack, moving up beside him. "Also in thinking I might talk sense to Overton. Mistakes I won't make again, Cap."

Cap marked the banked, staring hate in Overton's eyes. It was for him as well as for Carmack. He shook his head.

"I came with the same hope — to talk

sense to him. I see it is useless. Let's get out of here!"

When the door closed behind Hugh Carmack and Cap McChensey, Kirby Overton continued to stand, his face twisted with the violence of his thwarted anger and malevolent hate. He beat his hands on the desk top and spewed curses with an aimless, wild venom that made Riff Powers stare and then edge uneasily toward the door.

Overton paid Powers no attention, letting him go. But when Trace Furlong would have followed, Overton broke off his tirade of cursing.

"Wait!"

Furlong paused, got out tobacco and papers and built a cigarette.

"Well?"

"That thousand dollars we spoke of. Go out and earn it!"

"I had the chance when he was riding in," Furlong reminded. "It won't be that easy again. He'll be wary, now."

"No matter. The money's waiting for you."

Furlong took a deep drag at his cigarette, looked Overton up and down with a careful calculation. In the taut minute just passed, Trace Furlong had gained several impressions. One was that if Cap McChesney had not appeared as he had, and things gone on to a shootout, the smoke rolling would have been strictly between Carmack and himself. For, though Kirby Overton had hit at Carmack with words, he had been careful to make no move toward anything more lethal. Riff Powers was a question mark, also, willing to offer moral support, but show as a weak reed in a tough ruckus.

Furlong tipped a skeptical shoulder. "If the money is waiting, how about seeing half of it now, the rest when the chore is finished?"

Fresh anger flared in Overton's eyes, scalded his florid cheeks.

"You think I'd short change you?"

"No — I'd make sure that you didn't. But I'll be putting my skin on the line, and any man can stub his toe. Just in case, I want the chance to spend some of the money, first."

"I'm not paying you to get killed," blurted Overton.

"And I'm not exactly aiming to be," Furlong told him flatly. "But it could happen. I might miss, while Carmack wouldn't. So, five hundred now, the balance when the chore is finished."

"No!"

Furlong tipped a shoulder again.

"Takes a weight off my mind, not having

to go after him. Far as I'm concerned, Carmack can live to be a hundred."

Overton swung away from his desk.

"What the hell kind of talk is that? You trying to hold me up?"

"No. Just taking another look at how much my skin is worth to me."

"Maybe you're afraid?"

"Maybe. Or cautious. One thing sure, I can damn easy forget I have any quarrel with Long Seven or Hugh Carmack."

"Not if you ride for me, you can't!"

Furlong flipped away his cigarette butt. "We can fix that, too. You want to write my time?"

Overton, pacing angrily about the room, came to a quick stop. "Who said anything about writing your time?"

"I did," stated Furlong. "If that's the way you want it."

Overton threw up an arm in defeat. "Who said I wanted it?"

He turned to the corner cupboard, rummaged the rear of a shelf and came up with a small metal box. From this he took a sheaf of currency and counted out a packet of bills. He shoved these across to Furlong.

"I make that five hundred. Want to check it?"

Grinning crookedly, Furlong pocketed the money.

"Your count's good enough. Any particular time, place, or way you want me to earn it?"

Overton showed an impatient shrug. "The place and way are up to you. As for the time — the quicker, the better!"

Furlong moved to the door. "I'll be heading for town."

13

By the time Hugh Carmack rode in at Long Seven headquarters the wind had shifted and quieted, and while snow was still falling the blur of white flakes had thinned and day's deep gloom lessened. He put up his horse, racked his saddle and went into the bunkhouse, where Sam Hazle and Case Ivy had a warm fire going. They made way for him by the stove.

"Neal?" questioned Sam. "You get any more word?"

Carmack shook his head. "I'll be heading for town again, later on. Sam, the wind's changed and the snow's letting up some. While it slacks off is a good time for Bronco Charley and his people to get back into their rancheria cabins. How about riding out to

Midnight Butte with the word?"

"Damn right!" Sam said quickly. "I been feeling plenty guilty, sitting up to his warm stove and thinking about those people out in a brush camp. Like the papoose that grinned at us — that little mite of a critter, out in this kind of weather."

"Tell Bronco Charley he and his people will have to double up some, until they can put together some more cabins to make up for the ones Overton had torn down. But they'll still be better off than out in the brush."

"What if Overton tries another raid?" Case Ivy asked.

"He does," Carmack said, with a somber intensity, "I'll kill him. I just told him so. I've had a big plenty of Mister Kirby Overton for a long time. All of a sudden the jug is full and running over. Either he gets back in his own corral and stays there, or I hunt him down and call him — finally and for good!"

"Where'd you see him to tell him that?" Sam demanded.

"At Slash 88."

"You mean — you rode in there?"

"That's right."

"Wasn't using your head," scolded Sam.

"Wonder they didn't cut you down on sight!"

Carmack shrugged. "Water under the bridge."

Sam reached down his coat. "A long time ago we should have laid it on the line to Overton — laid it cold, like you just did. Things would have been different if we had. But, no — we had to give him first bite. You going to act that way foolish some more, you better wait until I get back, so I can hit for town with you."

"By the time you get back from Midnight Butte, you'll have had enough riding for one day," Carmack told him. "Besides, I may stay the night in town."

Sam left, well bundled against the weather, Carmack, driven by a sudden and ravenous hunger, sought the cook shack. A pot of stew simmered on the stove and he wolfed biscuits and two plates of this while draining the coffee pot.

The comforting lift of hot food brought a measure of relaxation and he spent a drowsy fifteen minutes over his final cup of coffee and a couple of cigarettes. Benjy Todd, lighting up a stubby, villainous pipe, sat down across the table from him.

"Sam and Case told me about Neal," Benjy said. "I'm fond of that boy. We lose him, I'm going to be mighty upset. I ain't hitched on a gun in thirty years, but I'm ready to."

Carmack surveyed him with a touch of grim amusement. The grizzled, waspy little cook would weigh all of a hundred and ten pounds with his pockets full of horseshoe nails. The spark in his eye, however, told of a spirit big enough to match the size of any man.

"Don't think that will be necessary, Benjy," Carmack told him. "Neal's in good hands. He's young and bull-strong. I think we'll keep him with us, all right."

Benjy sucked meditatively at his pipe.

"Funny how things shape up. Life runs along smooth as a man could wish. Then some damn fool gets maggots in his brain and starts stirring up trouble. Them kind is just born to need killin'. That feller Overton could be one of such."

"Yes," agreed Carmack. "He could be."

Half an hour later, up on a fresh horse, he headed down valley again. The wind had died and the snow ceased to fall, and a great stillness lay over the land. But the sky remained dark with storm and the Barrier Hills were shrouded with its threat. This, Carmack knew, was merely the pause before a heavier weather onslaught, which he hoped would hold off long enough for the Pomos to get back into their cabins.

All the way to town he saw neither man or beast, and town itself, when he rode in, had a chilled, huddled look, with ragged areas of snow spread on moisture darkened roofs and drifted against weathered walls. Wheel tracks the length of the street's slush told of the but lately arrived, twice-a-week stage. From every chimney wood smoke lifted, and, though full dark was still hours away, lamp light shone pallidly through moisture fogged windows.

He reined into the runway of Packy Devine's livery barn, found the place empty, so unsaddled and cared for his horse himself. Memory of what had taken place last night in this very spot struck sharply. But it was startling to realize how far that grim happening had already been pushed into the background by later events. Also startling was the realization that he felt no particular discomfort over the part he had played in the incident.

Evidently, he mused, in pursuing the right as he saw it, a man was invisibly armored against any lasting mental scar, no matter how grim or bitter the episode. A man did what his conscience told him he had to do. It was that simple. And all the argument in the world could not change that basic fact.

He tramped down street and turned into Lindermann's store, to inquire about the mail. Henry Lindermann had just finished sorting the scanty contents of a limp mail sack, and shook his head to Carmack's request.

"Nothing for you, Hugh. Damned little for anybody."

Carmack hooked a hip on the counter and rolled a cigarette.

"What's the latest word on Neal Burke?"

"Tip Marvin was in a little bit ago. Said Doc Blair claims Neal is more than holding his own."

Carmack nodded his relief.

"Henry, I sent Sam Hazle out to Midnight Butte with word for Bronco Charley and his Pomo folks to get back into their cabins again where they'll have decent shelter. With luck they could make it before the storm opens up again. But they lost a lot of stuff when Overton ran them out and it's bound to be slim pickings for them for a while. Some flour and beans and other odds and ends of grub will help like hell. I want you to have Packy Devine load up a spring wagon with such supplies tomorrow morning and haul it out to them. I'll foot the bill."

A pair of hanging lamps spread a yellow

glow through the store. In the light of these, Henry Lindermann stood, spare and shrewd. He studied Carmack out of shadowed eyes.

"Anybody would think you were under some kind of obligation to those Indians, Hugh."

Carmack drew deeply on his cigarette and the pale smoke winnowed about his lean face and head.

"Maybe I am, Henry. Maybe you are, too. Maybe all of us are. They were here first. When you come right down to it, anything any of us got was originally taken from them. So who are we now to deny them the right to decent shelter and food?"

Lindermann showed a small restlessness. "You wield a sharp prod," he grumbled, then added, "Kirby Overton doesn't seem to feel that way."

"He wouldn't," returned Carmack crisply. "We won't count him."

"Maybe you have to," Lindermann said. "The man is real. He exists. He's here, in this valley. He ran the Pomos off the strip once. He may do it again."

"Not if he knows what's good for him." A thread of harshness roughened Carmack's words. He dropped off the counter, headed for the door. "You'll take care of those supplies, Henry?"

"I'll take care of them. And, Hugh — I'll split the cost with you."

Carmack came around, quick warmth in his eyes.

"You don't have to, Henry. But it's damned decent of you to offer, just the same."

Lindermann shrugged. "It's settled. We split the cost. And I know Packy will be glad to do the hauling for nothing. This valley's been good to me. I've been here a long time. I expect to die here. I liked it the way it was, every part of it. I want to see it stay that way. And," he ended gruffly, "I approve completely how you handled the Hobey Beecham affair."

Leaving, Carmack met Bill Kyle at the door. Kyle was a man grown gruff and taciturn from years of long, solitary miles up on a jolting, swaying stage box. His greeting was a single word, "Hugh!" accompanied by a slap on the shoulder.

Carmack grinned briefly. "Another season of tough weather ahead, Bill. You ought to retire and sit by the fire."

"Hell with that!" growled the stage driver. "I wouldn't last the winter. I've lived too long on fresh air to do without it."

Carmack went on, crossing the street to

the Acme. Henry Lindermann moved up beside Kyle and nodded at Carmack's receding back.

"You're one of the real old ones, Bill. You knew his father, didn't you?"

Kyle nodded. "Old Buck Carmack? Sure, knew him well. Hugh's just like him. Solid. The kind that hold a country together."

"Yes," agreed Lindermann thoughtfully. "Yes."

In the Acme, Marty McGah and Packy Devine had a cribbage board between them. Carmack waved them up to the bar.

"Don't know why I should stand a drink for a pair of bums," he told Russ Herrick. "But I hate to drink alone." Then, as Marty and Packy fell in on either side of him, he went on. "How the devil do you two get by in the world without turning in at least an occasional lick of work?"

Marty chuckled. "Well, for one thing, we let kind souls like you buy our liquor for us."

"And take our eatin' money from anybody we can get into a game of stud or draw," Packy put in, his eyes twinkling.

Carmack slammed a palm on the bar. "That settles it. I've had a big plenty of your poker-playing brag. After supper, I'm tying into you. Before I'm done, you'll be begging for mercy."

Marty winked at Russ Herrick. "Now will you listen to the man!" He lifted his glass to Carmack. "Hughie, my boy, you've bought yourself a ruckus!"

They drank, then when Marty and Packy bought, drank twice more, all the while bickering and insulting each other amiably. Afterwards, when Russ Herrick would have set one up on the house, Carmack took a cigar instead and stowed it carefully away for his after supper smoke. The liquor had warmed and relaxed him and he drew a deep comfort from such casual moments with old and proven friends.

The afternoon ran away and as early twilight settled in, bleak and cold, the supper gong at the Mountain House sounded. Whereupon they left the Acme and headed for the hotel, with Marty McGah swearing softly as he tried to pick a reasonably dry way through the street's mud.

"Damn such weather!" he complained. "I'll always say Nature's biggest oversight was in not making man so he could curl up somewhere like a chipmunk in a hollow log and sleep the winter away."

"Change of seasons is good for you," Carmack countered.

"Not for me," Marty vowed. "Maybe I got

a touch of lizard blood in me, but I sure like to lie in the sun."

They climbed the steps of the Mountain House and Maude Lawrence met them at the door. She pointed to several gunny sacks spread on the porch and to a broom leaning against the wall.

"Use them," she ordered. "I'll not have my floors all tracked up."

"Ma'am," assured Marty McGah meekly, "we wouldn't think of such a thing."

So they scuffed and brushed boots and went in, Carmack pausing for a moment, an unspoken question in his glance.

Maude Lawrence nodded reassuringly. "He's sleeping, Hugh. And Doc Blair is quite cheerful."

"Fine!" Carmack dropped a hand on her arm. "My debt to you continues to grow."

"Nothing of the sort," she denied. "Just see that you stay healthy yourself."

A moment before, a rider had turned into the upper end of the street. At the jangling summons of the hotel gong he had reined up and watched Hugh Carmack and his two companions pick their way over the muddy street to the Mountain House. In spite of the thickening gloom he had no trouble identifying them. He waited until they disappeared into the hotel, then rode on to the livery stable. But short of the runway he hauled up once more and sat for a little time, staring at the door's wide rectangle of yawning blackness.

Last night a man had died in there — on the end of a rope. Cynical and ruthless as was his basic makeup, Trace Furlong owned to a streak of superstition. It was stirring in him now. And he decided that something of what had happened to Hobey Beecham, might rub off on a man if he rode in there. So he swung away, denying his horse the shelter of the stable, leaving the animal instead in the alley beside Lindermann's store. Here he spread his slicker across his saddle, then took another good look along the street.

He saw several other shadowy figures emerge from various doorways and head for the Mountain House. He would have liked to have gone there himself. But knowing from experience even under the best conditions the hostility Maude Lawrence felt toward him, the happenings of the past few days made it certain there would be no welcome for him in the hotel. So he crossed to the Acme.

Russ Herrick was alone and gave Furlong the briefest of nods. At this moment, Trace Furlong had more money in his pocket than ever before in his life, and it was crying to be spent. So he bought a sealed fifth of whiskey and carried it and a glass to one of the poker tables. After which he raided Russ Herrick's free lunch.

This food was plain but good, and the whiskey was smooth. Furlong put away plenty of both. Most men would have mellowed under the conditions, but Furlong was the sort in whom alcohol awakened a latent savagery and turned him quarrelsome and cruel. He took to watching Herrick and presently ripped out harsh, droning words.

"What the hell makes you so sour, Herrick? You afraid to talk?"

The saloon owner shrugged. "Nothing to say."

"Wasn't that way last night. Had something to say then, didn't you? Took Carmack's side and put in your dime's worth against Hobey Beecham. Bad habit of yours, Herrick — being partial to Carmack. Could get you in considerable trouble."

Russ Herrick had spent his adult lifetime behind a bar. He had seen them come and go and knew the many degrees of men's behavior under the drive of whiskey. He had listened to their talk and seen their actions, and knew when to argue with them and when to leave them alone.

Here he had watched a man put away several heavy jolts of hundred proof whiskey and knew how the effect of this could suddenly peak up and turn loose all that man's inhibitions. It was that way now with Furlong and hardly a time to argue. So Herrick kept his peace and resumed poring over a newspaper that had come in on the day's stage.

Furlong downed another drink. The whiskey was wildly alive in him and abruptly he cursed, pulled his gun and slammed it heavily on the table beside the whiskey bottle. He stared straight ahead at the door and all the couched malevolence in him showed in the glitter of his eyes and the set of his dark, narrow face.

Russ Herrick put his paper carefully aside. After all, you could ignore a drunk only so far. Then something had to be done about it. There were some who grew loose and clumsy and uncertain under a load of whiskey, but others, who had the real venom in them, could turn increasingly deadly up to the time the liquor finally won complete mastery and dropped them like a stroke. Trace Furlong was one of such.

Herrick tried some casual, carefully chosen words.

"Easy, Trace. Better put the gun away."

Furlong paid no attention, seemed not to hear. Yet, when Herrick would have shifted along behind the bar, Furlong caught up the weapon with an order that struck like a whiplash.

"Stay put!"

Herrick froze. This fellow, this Trace Furlong was plainly on the kill, and dangerous as a coiled rattler. He had brought a feral purpose into the Acme with him, secreting it carefully until, fed with whiskey, it was now suddenly blazing in the open.

On the kill for whom? From remarks Furlong had made a short time ago, it had to be one particular man — Hugh Carmack! And at any moment now, along with Marty McGah and Packy Devine, Carmark would be returning from supper for the promised poker game. When he stepped through that door, unsuspecting, he wouldn't have a chance.

Desperation gripped Russ Herrick.

On a shelf under the bar some six feet away rested an old, snub-nosed Bulldog six-shooter. It had been there a long time. It hadn't been fired in years, but it was loaded and ready to go. By dropping suddenly behind the bar, Herrick knew he could get hold of the gun all right. But after that, what to do?

He had never made claim to be any sort of a hand with a gun. Across the short width of a bar top, he might likely hit a man. But across the width of the room, where Trace Furlong now sat, he would far more likely miss. While Furlong would not!

From the street came the growl of men's voices and Marty McGah's laugh. Then, just beyond the closed door, it was Hugh Carmack saying:

"If you think to loot my pockets, Mister McGah, don't try any of your two pair bluffs. For I can read you like a book."

The door began to swing.

Russ Herrick dropped and dove for the old bar weapon. He gripped it, but did not try and come back up into the clear. Instead, he drove two slugs through the thin front of the bar in the general direction of Trace Furlong. And on the heels of the shots he yelled his warning.

"Hugh — look out, Hugh!"

Carmack had the door half open when the trapped echoes of the shots buffeted the room and Herrick's yell sounded. Reaction was automatic. Too far along to dodge back, he could only drive ahead then spin to one side, dragging at his gun. Out there in front of him was Trace Furlong, a gun in his hand, half turned toward the bar. The Slash

88 riding boss was caught slightly off balance and out of position, and knew it. He came whirling back, throwing a desperate, hurried shot at Carmack. It was too hurried, slamming into the wall inches away from Carmack's head.

Carmack fired across his twisting body. The bullet caught Furlong solidly and for a split second held him, reared high and stiff on his toes. Then his knees buckled, his shoulders caved, and he fell across the edge of the poker table, upsetting this and carrying it to the floor with him. He struck heavily and rolled over on his back.

Marty McGah and Packy Devine charged into the room, Packy empty handed, Marty with drawn gun.

"What is this?" Marty cried. "What is this?"

Russ Herrick came up from behind the bar, pale and sweating. His glance went from Furlong's sprawled figure to Hugh Carmack, then back to Furlong again. His hand shook as he dropped the snub-nosed gun on the bar and reached for a bottle and glass.

"This I need!" he mumbled.

Harshly still outside, but shaken within, Carmack looked down at Furlong. Marty McGah came up beside him, exclaiming again.

"This should surprise me all to hell — but it doesn't. And that fellow is still alive."

Trace Furlong coughed thickly. His eyes were open but held an unseeing stare. His lips moved and words came, choked and fading.

"Joke is — on Overton. You can — take the money. Because — I didn't — earn it!"

Carmack dropped to one knee. "What's this about money, Furlong? Money for what — ?"

Furlong did not answer.

Carmack got back to his feet and turned to Marty McGah.

"You heard him. What was he driving at?"

"Simple enough," Marty answered. "He was talking about money he didn't earn because you got him before he could get you."

"That's it!" vowed Russ Herrick. "That's it, Hugh. He was all set to drop you when you came through that door. Look at me — shaking like a leaf. Must be getting too old to stand this sort of thing. Man — I need another drink!"

Carmack moved over to the bar. "It was none of your mix, Russ. Yet you bought in. Why did you?"

Herrick threw up his hands.

"Hell, Hugh — I don't know. Guess I just

couldn't stand to see him cut you down without you having some kind of a break. All I did was grab this old bar gun of mine, let out a yell and cut loose with a couple of slugs through the front of the bar."

"Yes," said Carmack softly, "that's all you did. Thereby saving my skin. What can I say?"

"Nothing," blurted Herrick uncomfortably. "That's it — don't say this or that. It's all over. We were both lucky."

Carmack looked down at Trace Furlong again. "Packy," he said, "get Doc Blair."

Packy hurried away, soon to return, with Doc Blair at his heels. A middle aged man, spare and wiry, with thin, intelligent features, Doc Blair's examination was brief. He shrugged.

"I can't do him any good. Nobody can."

"Take a look in his pockets, Doc," Hugh Carmack directed. "He said something about money."

Doc came up with a handful of currency. He spread this on the bar, counting it.

"Close to five hundred dollars. A lot of money for such as Furlong to carry around. Where, I wonder, did he get it?"

"From Kirby Overton," put in Marty McGah bluntly. "That's blood money, Doc. A payoff for killing Hugh."

Doc Blair, a thoroughly decent man, stared at Marty, shocked.

"You can't mean that?"

"I sure as hell do!" Marty insisted. "Furlong as good as admitted it. Before he died he said the joke was on Overton. And that we could take the money because he didn't earn it. If that doesn't mean what I claim — what does it mean?"

Doc shook a regretful head. "I thought better of Kirby Overton than that." He indicated the money. "What's to do with that?"

"Use what you need to bury Furlong," Carmack said somberly. "Any that's left, we'll turn over to Bronco Charley and his people. They can put it to real good use."

14

Morning light crept across the world, furtive under a lowering sky that continued to threaten further storm. Flurries of rain around midnight had melted most of the previous day's snow, and only here and there remained a trace of it, banked soddenly against some obstruction. The Barrier Hills still brooded under heavy cloud cover and the wind off them was cold and damp.

Hugh Carmack had spent the night in the

Mountain House, lying long awake while adding up events and pondering again and again the cross purposes that could develop between men and tangle their lives. Grim and sobering thoughts they were, which slugged a man into a nerve-jaded weariness, and which held the indelible image of Trace Furlong and how he had looked as he violently lived and as violently died in his whiskey driven try to earn blood money . . .

It was full midnight before Carmack finally dropped off, mouth parched and bitter from the endless string of cigarettes he'd rolled and smoked. He woke feeling drained and stale, and not even one of Maude Lawrence's best breakfasts could cure his mood. It had helped some to look in at Neal Burke's room and receive Doc Blair's assurance that Neal's chances were looking better all the time.

On leaving town, however, instead of heading for the home ranch, Carmack took the trail for Gateway. For there would be waiting the swift, whole-hearted warmth of Kelly Logan's little girl trust and affection. These things would be his without reservation or doubt, and he had need of them to renew his faith and make his world whole and healthy again.

At Slash 88, Kirby Overton had made a

poor night of it, also, sitting alone in his office, waiting without success for Trace Furlong to return from town. It had been late when he turned in, restless and edgy with his thoughts. Up in the gray dawn's bleakness he dressed quickly, cursing the shivering chill and hurrying for the warmth of the cookshack. Here three of the crew were about to sit up to their breakfast. They eyed him uncertainly.

"Furlong?" he asked. "Did he get in last night?"

It appeared he did not.

Overton looked around. "Where's Powers?"

There was a drag of silence before grudging reply came.

"Don't know. Riff, he pulled out."

"Pulled out!" Overton stared at the speaker, lips thinning, his words sharp.

"That's it," shrugged the rider.

"When was this?"

"Long about nine o'clock last evening. He'd been sittin' around, quiet like. All of a sudden he's up and packin' his warbag. Didn't say why or where or anything. Just got his gear together and left."

Overton took a seat and the cook put breakfast in front of him. He ate and drank mechanically, touched with foreboding. Of all his crew, Trace Furlong and Riff Powers were the two in whom he had placed the most reliance. Now neither were at hand. Why?

Maybe, with the game growing increasingly stern, he was beginning to learn the true measure of men's allegiance. And it was hardly comforting!

Done with their meal the three crew members edged quietly out. As though, Overton thought bitterly, they too were uneasy and ready to run!

Alone at the table he sat long, searching his thoughts for answers. The defection of Riff Powers, now that he considered all facts fully, was not, in all truth, too much of a surprise. For during those taut moments in the office yesterday afternoon, Powers had shown himself to be a highly uneasy man, one who was openly relieved when Cap McChesney put in his unexpected appearance. Plainly, with the big chips down, Riff Powers had little stomach for gunplay.

Trace Furlong however, was another kettle of fish. Here was one who, while no reckless fool, did not scare easily. But he did own to a cold, twisted cynicism and a contempt for the accepted creed of human values which might easily lead him to forget a promise or sneer at any man's given word, including his own. So it could very well be that Trace Furlong, richer by five hundred dollars than ever before in his life, and with the footloose restlessness of his kind overly strong in him, had simply headed out for new country and new scenes. Still again, it was entirely possible that he was holed up in town somewhere, sleeping off a load of whiskey.

For a full hour Kirby Overton sat, turning these various conjectures over and over in his mind, while all the time the need for knowing something for sure, mounted in him. And the only way he'd know that something, was to ride to town himself. Convinced finally of this he left the cookshack and tramped back to the ranchhouse. Along the way he called an order to one of the crew.

"Put my saddle on that big trail horse of mine."

In the ranchhouse he strapped on a gun.

Riding the east side trail for Gateway and coming up to the Middle Ford of Warrior Creek, Hugh Carmack reined in and laid a glance all about him. Here was stillness, save for the voiceless lisp and murmur of the stream. Along its banks the willows and alders spilled thinning leaves that were touched with late season color. East and west across the run of the valley an occasional rank of conifers reared in darker tone, and on an up-thrust snout of lava close by, a solitary clump of aspens brightened this somber world with a defiant smear of flame.

Reaching further with his survey, Carmack considered the Slash 88 headquarters looming yonder across the middle distance. Even under these dull skies the big ranchhouse gleamed whitely, thrusting its arrogant presence across the land. Little activity was in evidence about the place, with but a single man in view, saddling a horse by the corrals. Then Kirby Overton showed, crossing from the ranchhouse. And it was he who swung up on the horse and came directly on toward the creek ford.

He came at a run, his horse fretting with morning spirit, slowing only at the water's edge to enter at a splashing trot. Then Hugh Carmack, dropping past a screen of willow, also rode into the stream. Here he reined up, watching Overton in cold silence.

Hauling in abruptly, Overton swung high and forward in his stirrups, and for several taut and strumming moments these two men, implacable in their enmity, faced each other across the chill expanse of sliding water. Carmack finally spoke, his words falling with a sort of detached quietness far more ominous than a shout would have been.

"You know, Overton, I sometimes think the lives of all of us are fated, our trails charted, the time and place of our endings fixed. But whether or not that be so, this is as it should be. Just the two of us, here now to settle everything. You agree?"

Overton eased slowly back into his saddle. He tried to find something to say, but no words came. And Carmack went on in the same quiet, deadly way.

"You're minus another man, Overton. Last night in town, Trace Furlong had a big try at killing me. He didn't quite get there. Before he died, he said the joke was on you because he didn't earn the money you paid him. Blood money, Overton — that was what he was talking about. Money you paid him to kill me. Yes, blood money. And when a man lowers himself to the point where he's willing to pay blood money, then he sure as hell is a long way down. Also — too dangerous to let run loose any longer . . . I told you how it would be if you didn't get back into line and stay there. I guess you didn't believe me. So — here and now, Overton — here and now!"

Quickening fear grew in Overton. Here

no meeting of words where words would suffice. This was it!

Trace Furlong! For all his swagger and talk, just a blundering fool, after all. . . . Yet, maybe he wasn't too much at fault. Maybe it just wasn't in the cards for anyone to ever best this fellow Carmack. Maybe what he'd just said about fate was so, with fate all on his side . . .

If only Furlong hadn't said anything about money. But for that, maybe talk would have been enough. Maybe it still was. Kirby Overton drew a thin breath and tried some.

"Furlong lied, Carmack. I paid him no money and he had no orders from me to go after you; if he tried, it was his own private grudge. The facts are, after you and Cap McChesney left yesterday, I got to thinking about your offer — that we call it quits. The more I thought of it the more it made sense. So I'm willing to meet you half way and — ."

Carmack shook his head, cutting in.

"Won't do, Overton. Furlong didn't lie. But you're lying now. The truth isn't in you and I wouldn't trust you out of my sight ever again. There's no point in further talk. Get at it while I'm still willing to give you the even break you'd never offer me. God damn it — you heard what I said — get at it!"

The final words were a ringing harshness, and now it was Carmack who was poised high and forward-leaning and ready.

In Kirby Overton, quickening fear peaked to desperation. There was no way out. Right here, right now, a lifetime of hate and enmity must be resolved, one way or another. This man in front of him — lean, implacable — this Hugh Carmack — opposing him as always, beating him back — once more blocking his way — !

Desperation turned to blind, badgered rage. It boiled up with a crazy suddenness out of hidden, long-smoldering depths into which no one save Overton himself had ever fully peered. It turned his florid cheeks hectic, it swelled the cords of his throat and congested his eyes with madness. It even found vocal utterance, bursting from him in a hoarse unintelligibility that was half growl, half frenzied yell. Cruelly yanked reins and a lifting, savage slash of spur rowels brought his horse up, rearing high and wild, front legs flailing and scattering water. And Overton went for his gun.

For all his watchful alertness, Hugh Carmack was caught somewhere off balance by the very intensity of Overton's explosive reaction, and only the fact that the upthrown head of that frantically rearing horse threw a momentary barrier between its rider and himself, gave him time to free his own gun.

Overton tried for Carmack past that tossing equine head, but the margin of target was too narrow and not fully clear. He missed. The smash of report so close to its ears, sent the horse into another rearing whirl, and Overton's second try was fired during this unstable, dizzying spin. The slug, a little low and wide, slashed into the swell fork of Carmack's saddle.

When Overton's horse came down again on all four feet, it and its rider were split second still. Carmack, watching carefully, drove a single, coldly deliberate shot.

Kirby Overton hunched, then bowed far forward along the neck of his horse, face buried in its tossing mane while the animal lunged back to the far bank. As the horse gained this, Overton slithered from his saddle, loose and headlong. He landed on the hoof-gouged gravel, his boots trailing in the water.

Hugh Carmack quieted his own mount and watched for a little time. Then he rode through the hurrying stream, past Overton's crumpled figure, and on to Slash 88 headquarters.

The echo of the shots had carried and now, gathered at the corrals were three punchers who watched Carmack's approach with guarded eyes and blank faces. Carmack, reining up, gave them the word curtly.

"Overton's down there at the ford. It was an even break. Also, Trace Furlong won't ever be back." He let the full significance of these blunt statements sink in before adding: "Is this thing finished? If it isn't, let's hear about it — now!"

One of the three shrugged. "Far as I'm concerned, it's finished. It was never my row."

The other two agreed that it wasn't theirs, either.

"Good enough," Carmack said. "That suits me."

He reined away and they watched him go, back to the ford and across it and on past the willows beyond.

At Gateway it was baking day again and Sherry Gailliard had a small helper in Kelly Logan. Both were happy in their companionship, which held a deepening intimacy that was very comforting. Kind and motherly as Maude Lawrence was when Kelly stayed with her at the Mountain House in town, the very size of the hotel, with its many demands and activities, denied it the home-like atmosphere of this warm and savory ranchhouse kitchen.

It was Kelly who glanced from a window and saw Carmack riding in past the corrals.

"Uncle Hugh!" she cried, racing with eagerness to the door.

Sherry, brushing flour from her hands, watched him leave his horse and come on. His hat was pulled low and he moved as though stiffly weary. When Kelly burst from the door, he caught her up and held her with an intensity of feeling that startled even the child. In return she hugged him with all her small strength.

Past Kelly's dark head, Sherry met Carmack's glance and saw the ragged shadow in his eyes. She exclaimed.

"Hugh! What is it?"

He shook his head slightly. "Later."

He sat in the kitchen, hunched over a cup of coffee. His hair was tousled and awry and a bristle of whiskers roughened his cheeks. The pull of some inner tension made his jaw-line stand out hard and edged. And the shadow in his eyes hung on, even as he listened to Kelly's eager chatter and managed a grave smile or two.

Presently, from the living room, old Jeff Gailliard made gruff call for Kelly, who danced away in answer. Immediately, Sherry stood before Carmack.

"All right," she said. "Now tell me."

He drew a deep breath. "Overton," he said. "I just killed him."

Sherry paled slightly, but she did not flinch. After a moment of stillness she spoke steadily.

"I knew it must be something like that. How did it happen, and where?"

"At Middle Ford. I met up with him there on my way from town. It was an even shake. Last night in town it was Trace Furlong making a try for me in the Acme. In his pocket he had five hundred dollars which Overton had paid him to kill me. My luck held up. Furlong's didn't. After that I knew what I had to do."

Carmack spoke in a monotone, his words flat and without inflection, all the while staring straight ahead. Now he looked up to meet her eyes.

"Yes, in town it was Furlong who started it. But at Middle Ford, I did. I called Overton — I made him fight. And I killed him. Now, Sherry — for you and me — there can't be any use —."

His words trailed off. He shook his head, picked up his hat from the floor and got to his feet, prepared to leave.

Standing very straight, Sherry blocked his way.

"What do you mean — there can't be any use for you and me? How — how do you know?"

"I just told you what I did. I killed Trace Furlong and I killed Kirby Overton. Furlong probably wouldn't ever count. But Overton — that would always be between us. You'd never be able to forget about Overton. So — !" He shrugged wearily.

"Foolish man!" She said it gently. "I've already forgotten. Oh, I'm not callous, but I am a realist. I've long dreaded that one day things would come to just such a pass as this. There was an inevitability about it. Now that it has happened, all that counts is that it is you who are here, alive and safe. Oh, Hugh — !" Her lips quivered and the sudden brilliance of tears was in her eyes.

Carmack stared, fighting disbelief. He reached and caught her by the shoulders, shook her gently.

"Girl, do you realize what you're saying — what it sounds like you mean — ?"

She nodded quickly, a smile breaking past the tears.

"Of — of course I realize what I'm saying — and I mean exactly what it sounds like I mean. We'll probably fight a lot, like always.

But — but that won't really matter, will it?"

"No," he said, "that won't matter — it won't matter a bit. Just so there's you and me and Kelly — and the whole great damn wonderful world . . . !"

We hope you have enjoyed this Large Print book. Other Thorndike, Wheeler, Kennebec, and Chivers Press Large Print books are available at your library or directly from the publishers.

For information about current and upcoming titles, please call or write, without obligation, to:

Publisher
Thorndike Press
295 Kennedy Memorial Drive
Waterville, ME 04901
Tel. (800) 223-1244

or visit our Web site at:

http://gale.cengage.com/thorndike

OR

Chivers Large Print
published by BBC Audiobooks Ltd
St James House, The Square
Lower Bristol Road
Bath BA2 3SB
England
Tel. +44(0) 800 136919
email: bbcaudiobooks@bbc.co.uk
www.bbcaudiobooks.co.uk

All our Large Print titles are designed for easy reading, and all our books are made to last.